Learning To Fly

Howard Martin

ISBN-13: 9798620556977

Cover image by Fidelity Design and Print, Unit 7, Kenneth Way, Wilstead Industrial Park, Bedford, MK45 3PD, UK, Tel: +44 (0)1234 907907

CHAPTER ONE

'What are you doing today, Roger?' asked Alison, her gimlet eyes focused on Roger's face.

'Oh, I thought I'd go to Linton Airfield to see about some flying lessons,' answered Roger somewhat defensively, studiously avoiding the stare.

Alison frowned, her brow furrowed like a freshly ploughed field. 'Oh no, Roger. No. I thought we had discussed this and decided against it?'

'No dear. We discussed it, and you decided against it,' retorted Roger 'That's quite different.'

Alison's furrows grew deeper. 'I thought we ruled it out on the grounds of cost. Flying is a costly hobby.'

Roger took a deep breath. 'Flying is expensive, yes, but you know it's been my life's ambition. I've wanted to learn to fly ever since I was a kid. Dad left me the money in his will for that specific purpose if you remember.'

He picked up his cup of tea, hoping this would settle the argument in his favour.

Alison had other ideas. 'Yes, so you said. But that was before you married me. You have other responsibilities now. I need that money to build an extension, so Mother can come and live with us.'

Roger sprayed his tea in all directions and started to choke.

He didn't like Alison's Mother, who never stopped bitching about the lack of grandchildren, darkly hinting that Roger was to blame.

He regained some composure. 'No. Never. Over my dead body.'

'Well, that's a bit drastic, but I could arrange it, I suppose.'

'I think I would rather be dead than have your mother living here. There must be an old peoples' home somewhere in the world that would be prepared to take her. A war zone perhaps? Iraq? Afghanistan?'

'Very funny, Roger,' said Alison 'If we built a granny flat on the side of the house, it would be self-contained. You wouldn't know she was there until she needed something.'

'What, like an argument, you mean?' Roger felt he was starting to get the upper hand.

'No Roger, I didn't,' replied Alison 'I meant that Mother isn't getting any younger, and shouldn't be living on her own. She's forever falling over.'

'Tell her to take more water with it then,' said Roger 'drinking neat whisky at her age is bound to cause problems.'

'Oh, you are impossible, Roger,' said Alison 'I'm off to work. Now forget your silly idea of learning to fly. I've decided we'll use your Father's money for the extension. If you want my co-operation in the bedroom, you'll think very carefully about what I've said.'

'What co-operation?' spluttered Roger 'I could have more fun in a bloody funeral parlour; well assuming I got to the body before rigor-mortis set in. Otherwise, it'd be just like home!'

Alison glared at him, got up and slammed the door as she left. BANG!

Well, that shut you up, you old harridan, thought Roger. *Dad left that money for me to learn to fly, not for you to bring that old witch into our house.*

CHAPTER TWO

Roger grabbed his car keys and left the house. He climbed into his Mercedes S Class and surveyed his property. It was detached and stood in a reasonably sized plot of land that certainly would allow for the addition of a granny flat. Roger shuddered at the thought.

He started the car and drove off. Linton aerodrome was not far away, and often they heard the buzz of light aircraft flying over the house. Luckily, the main runway ran parallel to his road, so they were seldom disturbed by the larger aeroplanes unless the wind was coming from the airport direction.

Five minutes later, Roger drove up the approach road and turned off at the top on to the lane that ran around the perimeter. He paused briefly to read the signboard outside the flying club. "Linton Flight Training. Chief Flying Instructor, Michael Hunt".

Roger pulled into the car park and noted the row of light aircraft sitting on the other side of a chain-link fence. He smiled to himself as he felt his lifelong ambition take one step nearer. He got out of his car and approached the old hangar that housed the club.

'Can I help you, Sir?' Roger let the door go and stepped into the hangar. There was a small reception area with a counter, some seating and three doors that led off to other parts of the hangar. He looked around to see who had greeted him. It was an attractive middle-aged lady wearing a low-cut top which revealed rather too much of her ample bosom. Unfortunately, the lower half of her body was hidden by the counter.

'Err, I'm not sure. I want to learn to fly?' stuttered Roger, trying to look at her face rather than her breasts.

'In that case, you'll need a chat with our Chief Flying Instructor, Michael Hunt. Would you like me to find him for you?' she replied.

Roger finally managed to wrench his eyes upwards to her face and was pleasantly surprised to find that was quite attractive as well. She had long blond hair and a distinct glint in her eye.

'Yes please, err??' Roger liked the glint.

'Mandy, I'm Mandy. I look after reception and work in the bar. And you are?'

'I'm Roger, Roger Moore.'

'Roger Moore? Oh, is that your name or your ambition?' asked Mandy breathlessly.

'Err it's my name of course.'

'Oh, that's a shame, a real shame,' said Mandy disappointedly 'No relation to the other--'.

Roger cut her short. 'No. None at all. Everybody asks me that.'

Mandy picked up the phone. Roger heard a phone ring behind one of the three doors but which one? Roger guessed the middle. 'Hello, Mike? Mandy here. I've got a gentleman in reception who would like to learn to fly. OK.'

She put the phone down. 'He'll be right out.'

The middle door opened, and a small, balding man emerged. Roger was pleased his hearing was spot on.

'Oh, here comes Mike now,' said Mandy 'Mike, this is Roger Moore. Mr Moore, this is Michael Hunt, our Chief Flying Instructor.'

'Hello, Mr Moore, what can we do for you?'. Michael beamed a broad smile and held out his hand.

Roger was surprised that Michael had a strange drawl in his voice. 'Er, I'd like to learn to fly, please.'

'Well, you've definitely come to the right place. Come into my office, and we'll have a chat.' Michael turned on his heel and returned to his office. Roger followed behind, thinking Michael sounded more like the archetypal train spotter than a flying instructor.

'Come in, come in, Mr Moore. Take a seat. Now tell me, why do you want to learn to fly? Not thinking of doing it for a living are you?' Michael sat down, rested his chin on his hand, and stared expectantly at Roger.

'No, not really. It's been a life long ambition, but mainly for fun, I thought.'

'Just as well Mr Moore, just as well,' said Michael gloomily. 'I think the days of airline pilots are numbered due to advances in technology. They do say that in the future, the flight crew of an airliner will consist of one pilot and a dog.' He stared at Roger expectantly again.

Roger was confused. 'Sorry I--'

'The pilot will be there to feed the dog Mr Moore,' Michael interjected.

Roger was even more confused. 'Err, and the dog?'

'And the dog Mr Moore, will be there to bite the pilot if he looks like he's going to touch any of the controls!' Michael burst into laughter, sounding like a demented sea lion.

'Oh, right. Hilarious,' lied Roger.

'Yes, indeed Mr Moore, the creep of technology, is doing away with so many jobs. Luckily I think I may get away with it.'

'And why is that?'

'Well, can you imagine being taught to fly by a robot, Mr Moore?' Michael adopted a robotic voice. 'When I say to you —- YOU HAVE CONTROL -- you put your hands and feet lightly but positively on the controls and then say -- I HAVE CONTROL. When I wish to regain control, I will say -- I HAVE CONTROL. You will relinquish control and say -- YOU HAVE CONTROL.'

Roger was stunned. Michael quickly regained his composure. 'I'm so sorry, Mr Moore, I got quite carried away there. Now moving swiftly on, I would suggest a trial lesson to see how you take to flying? I'm free for the next hour, the weather is fine, so how are you fixed? Are you ready to spread your wings?'

This was the moment Roger had looked forward to for many years. 'Yes! Yes! I've nothing to do for the rest of the day so yes, let's do it.'

'Good man, good man,' said Michael.

They left the office and walked back through reception. Mandy was still standing behind the counter, and her nether regions remained a mystery. *Damn,* thought Roger.

'Oh Mandy, I'm taking Mr Moore for a trial lesson,' said Michael 'Can you book us out in Hotel-Tango, please?'

'Will do, Mike,' replied Mandy 'Hope you get it up OK, Mr Moore.'

Roger spun around, 'Err sorry, Mandy?'

Mandy lent forward on to the counter, displaying her cleavage. She gave Roger a wink. 'The aircraft, Mr Moore. I hope you get it up in the air, OK.'

'Oh, I see. Thanks, Mandy.' Roger returned the wink and closed the door behind him.

CHAPTER THREE

'Mandy, she seems very friendly?'
observed Roger as he and Michael walked
over the grass towards a row of light aircraft.

'Yes Mr Moore, she does,' replied Michael
'Over friendly, one might say. If one was
being unkind, one might say she was a
nymphomaniac. Randy Mandy, we call her.
Husband problem I think, probably not up
to the job. Take no notice. She tries it on with
everyone. Quite often succeeds as well.'

'Oh, I see. Has she tried it on with you?'

'Yes, she has Mr Moore. Without success, I
might add,' Michael raised his hand and
pointed to a wedding ring on his finger,
'Happily married man. Promised to another.
But perhaps we shouldn't be too hard on the

girl. Apparently, her first experience of sex was rape.'

Roger was visibly shocked 'Oh no, that's absolutely awful.'

Michael nodded his head in agreement 'Indeed, it was, Mr Moore. Indeed, it was. Luckily, the poor chap didn't press charges.'

CHAPTER FOUR

Roger stood next to the aircraft. It was much smaller than he had imagined. Michael saw the surprised look on his face. 'Rather compact, isn't it Mr Moore? But quite adequate for our purpose. This is a Cessna 152. This is Hotel-Tango. Light aircraft are generally referred to by the last two letters of their registration, in this case, HT, and we use the phonetic alphabet for clarity, hence Hotel-Tango.'

Roger said nothing. He was still stunned at seeing the aircraft close up.

'Now Mr Moore, the first thing to do is to check the aeroplane out, make sure it is safe to use. Please follow me around and see what I do, and I'm sure you will soon pick it up. So first we walk around the aeroplane and make sure there is no damage, nothing hanging off.'

They walked around the aeroplane and Roger resisted the temptation to joke about the rudder or elevators being loose, quite expecting it to be part of Michael's patter.

'Next, we check the oil in the engine by checking the level on the dipstick,' Michael opened a small flap on the engine 'notice that it screws in and out, not like a car. Yes, that seems sufficient. Next, we would check the contents of the fuel tanks to ensure we've got ample fuel for our intended flight, but I refuelled it myself earlier on, so we'll just check the gauges inside. OK get in Mr Moore, no, no, the left-hand seat please, that is the pilot's seat.'

Roger climbed in. 'Not much room,' he said taking a deep breath in.

'No, not a lot. You certainly need to be friends. Now put these headphones on, and I'll start the engine and call Air Traffic Control.'

'CLEAR PROP!' Michael shouted then turned the key, and after a few revs, the engine burst into life.

'The engine has started, so check oil pressure is on the rise' Michael pointed at the oil pressure gauge 'Looking good. Now I'll call Air Traffic for clearance to taxi to the runway.'

Michael pressed a button on the control column. 'Linton Tower, Hotel-Tango. Request taxi for a local flight.'

'Roger Hotel-Tango.' Roger was surprised how clear it was in his headphones. 'Cleared taxi for the holding point for runway Two Six, QNH One Zero One Five.'

Michael pressed the button again 'Cleared to the holding point for runway Two Six, One Zero One Five, Hotel-Tango.'

Michael turned to Roger, 'Now Mr Moore, we set One Zero One Five on the sub-scale of the altimeter. This will then read our altitude above sea level. We press on the top of the rudder pedals to release the brakes, increase power on the engine and hey presto we're moving. Note if I press the right rudder pedal we start to turn right, and if I press the left rudder pedal we start to turn left. Your turn now, practise turning left and right as we taxi towards the runway. You have control.'

'I have control,' said Roger. He pressed on the left rudder pedal and was pleased that the aircraft did indeed turn to the left. He tried the right rudder pedal, and yes the aircraft turned to the right. *Wow, nothing to this flying lark* he thought.

Michael was pleased, as well. 'Now we are approaching the holding point for runway Two Six so use your toes to press both pedals gently at the top to apply the brakes. OK, well done. Now I have control. I'll perform the take-off checks, and the power checks, and we'll be ready to go.'

Michael took control and ran the engine up and then checked various gauges, muttering to himself as he did. *Perhaps it's not so simple* Roger thought.

'OK Mr Moore, we are ready to go.' Michael pressed the button again 'Linton Tower, Hotel-Tango ready for take-off.'

'Hotel-Tango roger. Cleared take-off runway 26, the wind is Two Seven Zero degrees at One Zero Knots. Call for re-join.' Linton Tower came through loud and clear.

'Cleared take-off runway 26, Hotel-Tango' replied Michael 'Now Mr Moore, put your hands lightly on the control column and follow me through as we take off.'

Roger put his hands on the control column as Michael manoeuvred the aircraft on to the runway. He pushed the throttle lever forward, the engine sprang to life, and Roger found himself racing down the runway.

Michael pointed to the airspeed indicator 'When we reach about 60 to 65 knots we pull back on the control column and hey presto we are airborne!'

Roger watched the ground disappearing below him. He looked around, trying to get his bearings. They had taken off on the westerly runway, which meant his house would be on his left. He was busy looking for it when Michael interrupted. 'Now we level off at 1500 feet. We pick an attitude looking out the front window with the nose just below the horizon, wait for the speed to reach 90 knots and reduce to cruise power at 2200rpm by pulling back on the throttle. I'll trim the aircraft for straight and level flight. Now we'll look at the effects of controls. First, the elevators. Push the column forward, and the nose goes down and the speed increases. Pull the column towards you and the nose comes up and the speed decreases. Back to level flight. Now the ailerons. Turn the control column to the left, and the left wing drops and the right wing comes up. We are turning left. Now turn the control column to the right, and the right wing drops and the left wing comes up. We are turning right. Your turn now. You have control.'

'I have control,' acknowledged Roger and put his hands back on the control column. He was in charge of the aeroplane, he was flying, at last. Turning the control column to the left caused the aircraft to turn to the left. Turning it to the right caused the aircraft to turn to the right. Forward and backward movement also produced the required results. *This is easy* he thought.

'Well you seem to have the hang of that, Mr Moore,' said Michael 'so we'll head back to Linton. I have control. I'll call Linton for re-joining instructions.'

'Linton Tower, Hotel-Tango to the west, One Thousand Five Hundred feet on One Zero One Five, request re-join.'

'Roger Hotel-Tango. Join Left Hand Downwind for Runway Two Six, QFE Niner Niner Eight.'

'Left Hand Downwind for Runway 26, QFE Niner Niner Eight. Hotel-Tango.' Michael turned to Roger 'So we set Nine Nine Eight on the subscale of the altimeter, Mr Moore so that it now indicates our height above the runway threshold. Now, where is the airport?'

Roger looked around 'Yes, I can see it,' he said, pointing through the windscreen.

'OK,' said Michael 'We've been instructed to join left hand downwind for runway 26, so we need to fly parallel with the runway about half a mile south. That industrial estate makes a good point to aim for. You have control.'

'I have control,' said Roger. He gingerly moved the control column to keep the nose of the aircraft pointing at the industrial estate which seemed to be coming up very quickly.

'Excellent, Mr Moore,' said Michael 'Now I have control. Just watch what I do from now on in. Linton Tower, Hotel-Tango downwind.'

'Roger Hotel-Tango. Cleared land Two Six, QFE Niner Niner Eight, wind Two Seven Zero Six Knots', came the reply.

When the runway was disappearing behind them, Michael banked the aircraft to the left and looking through the side window, Roger began to recognise the streets below. Eventually, his own house came into view, looking like a model in a toy village.

Michael banked the aircraft left again and there in front of them was the runway they had taken off from. Thirty seconds later the wheels touched the ground, and they taxied back to the club.

CHAPTER FIVE

Michael and Roger walked back from the aircraft and entered reception.

'So, Mr Moore, your first flying lesson. A bit short perhaps, but what do you think?'

'Excellent! I really enjoyed it.'

'So will you be continuing on the path to a PPL? A Private Pilot's Licence?'

'Oh, absolutely!'

'I'm pleased to hear it, Mr Moore, pleased to hear it. Well, that was twenty minutes chock to chock time. I must go now, so I'll leave you in the capable hands of Mandy who will invoice you and book some more lessons. OK, Mandy?'

'OK Mike, will do.'

'Well, goodbye all.' Michael locked the till and left.

'Now Mr Moore, can you--'

'Mandy, please call me Roger. Mr Moore was my Father.'

Mandy smiled sweetly at Roger. 'OK, Roger. So twenty minutes chock to chock, oh and you'll need a logbook to record your hours, and here's our booklet about learning to fly, oh and a checklist for a Cessna One Five Two. Now, here is Mike's diary so you can book yourself in for some lessons while I complete your invoice.'

Roger thumbed through the diary and made some bookings. 'What happens if the weather is bad when I've got a lesson booked?'

'You need to do a lot of ground school. Air Law, Meteorology, Navigation etc. Read the 'Learning to Fly' book for more details. Now here's your invoice.'

Roger looked at the invoice. He removed some notes from his wallet and handed them to Mandy.

Mandy's face dropped. 'Oh, cash. Mike's gone now, and he's locked the till. Never mind, I'll put it somewhere safe where no one can get their hands on it.'

She tucked the wad of notes down her cleavage.

Roger laughed and shook his head. 'I thought you said you were going to put it somewhere safe where no one could get their hands on it.'

Mandy gasped then burst into laughter. 'Oh, you naughty boy! Look, if you are going to learn to fly here, you should join the flying club bar. Lots of other students you can talk to, and also the airline crews come in, so plenty of people to give you help and advice. The bar is on the opposite side of the road. There's also one extremely attractive barmaid as well.'

'Attractive barmaid, eh? That sounds good. Tell me her name, and I'll keep an eye out for her.'

'Her name is Mandy,'

'Well, what a coincidence,' said Roger keeping a straight face 'Two Mandys working so close together.'

'It's me, you idiot,' said Mandy in frustration.

'I know! I was just teasing. I'll go over and join now.'

Mandy grinned 'Go on. Out of my sight you. I'll be over to start my shift shortly.'

Talking of sight thought Roger *is Mandy glued behind that bloody counter?*

Roger pretended to make a fuss when he picked up his books, dropping one on the floor. 'Oh drat, could you open the door for me please, Mandy?'

Mandy and emerged from behind the counter. 'Of course, I can Roger.'

Roger stood and watched as she walked to the door.

Wow, he thought. *She's definitely got a spanner bum.*

Roger walked to the door. 'See you later, Mandy?'

Mandy smiled. 'Can't wait.'

CHAPTER SIX

Roger left reception, went to his car and put his books inside. Then he walked across to the flying club bar and entered.

The door opened into an empty lobby. As Roger stood there looking lost, an elderly man walked past.

'Can I help you?' the man asked gruffly.

'Oh yes. I wanted to join the club?'

'And why on earth would you want to do that?'

'Oh, I started to learn to fly today. Mandy from the school recommended I come over and join.'

The man smiled broadly. 'Oh right, do come in. Sorry about the gruff welcome, but I like to keep the bar membership only for the flying community. I have a late licence, and that attracts the wrong sort of person. What's your name?'

'It's Roger. Roger Moore.'

'Oh, any relation to--'

'None.'

'I'm Jed. It's my club, although perhaps not for much longer. Give me a tenner, go and get a drink, and I'll bring your membership card in later.'

Roger got out his wallet and handed Jed a ten-pound note. 'Thanks. I'll do that.'

Roger walked through the door into the main bar. There were groups of airline crews in uniform and several other people sitting around a large table. Roger walked to the bar.

'Hello, sir, can I help you?' asked the barman.

'Is Mandy here yet?'

The barman eyed the clock behind the bar. 'Well she should be, but I expect she has got held up in the Flight Training Centre. Can I get you a drink?'

'I'll have a pint of bitter please.'

'Certainly, Sir.' He picked up a glass and started to pour a pint.

A man appeared at the bar holding some empty glasses. He looked at Roger. 'Hello, I haven't seen you here before.'

'No,' replied Roger 'I only started learning to fly today.'

'Oh, good man. Come and join us over there on that table. We are all pilots. I'm George, and you are?'

'I'm Roger. Roger Moore.'

'Oh, any relation to--'

'No. None at all.'

George turned to the barman. 'Dave, can you put Roger's pint on my tab and bring us another round, please? Roger, come and meet the guys.'

George took Roger over to a table where a group of men was sitting. 'Guys, this is Roger. He's had his first flying lesson today. Roger, this is Martin, Alan and Guy.'

'Hi,' said Roger 'You all seem a friendly bunch of people.'

'One is delighted to make one's acquaintance,' said Guy in a Prince Charles voice.

'Oh give it a rest, Guy,' said Martin 'Sorry Roger, Guy thinks he's Prince Charles. Well, he's a Prince Charles Impersonator anyway. Tends to live the part.'

Roger pretended to be impressed. 'That must be quite interesting Guy, well apart from shagging the horse!'

'Please don't encourage him, Roger. We have to live with it.'

Roger sat down. 'So you are all pilots, are you?'

'Yes, we've all got licences except Guy,' said George 'he's the club's resident DJ and does the disco on Friday and Saturday nights.'

Dave, the barman, appeared with a round of drinks and proceeded to hand them out.

CHAPTER SEVEN

'So did you all--what the??' Roger exclaimed as something landed on his back. He twisted around. Mandy had crept up behind him and was resting one of her breasts on each of his shoulders.

'Hi, Roger. Jed asked me to give you your membership card.'

'Oh, thank you, Mandy. For a moment there, I thought I had turned into a camel.'

'Mandy smiled 'I'll be behind the bar if you need anything.'

'Anything?'

'Anything!'

'I see you have already met Mandy then,' said George.

'Yes. She seems to have taken a shine to me.'

'Don't flatter yourself mate. We've all been there.'

'What all of you?'

'I haven't,' said Guy 'I'd give my right arm to shag her.'

'But if you lost your right arm Guy, you'd have no sex life at all, would you?' remarked Alan.

'Yes, she's quite a lass. If you fancy her, then go for it' said George 'Her husband can't keep up with her, apparently.'

'Yes, that's what Michael said. So how long have you all been coming here, just since you learnt to fly?'

'Yes, it some years now' replied George 'there's so much fun that goes on in here. Jed used to own it all, the flight training and this bar, but he sold the flight training to an accountant a couple of years ago with an option on this bar. Jed told me the accountant now wants to take up the option.'

'Oh right, that makes sense,' said Roger 'I met Jed earlier on. He was quite hostile when I said I wanted to join the club until I said I was learning to fly. Then he couldn't have been more helpful. He did say he might not be the owner for much longer.'

'Yes, Jed has always been very protective of what we have here,' said George 'he has a late licence because the airline crew often fly back in late and want drink and food. He fears the accountant will take advantage of the licence and open membership up to all and sundry to make a quick buck. But that would be the death of this place.'

'Yes, I see what you mean,' Roger stood up 'look let me get you guys another round in. What are you all drinking?'

'Oh, ask Dave to do another round,' said George 'he's got a photographic memory.'

Roger made his way to the bar. Mandy spotted him and came over. 'Hello Roger, what can I do for you?'

'I'll tell you that later,' whispered Roger.

Mandy's eyes lit up. 'Ooh promises, promises.'

Roger smiled 'But for now, I'd like another round of drinks for the table over there, please. Dave knows the details.'

Mandy turned to Dave. 'Dave, can you do another round for Roger please?'

'You are on the table with George, aren't you?' asked Dave.

'Yes' replied Roger 'could you bring them over again, please? I'll pay Mandy.'

Roger took some notes from his wallet and gave them to Mandy. Mandy went over to the till and punched some numbers in, then sprang to one side as the draw shot open, narrowly missing her breasts. She remained at the side of the till as she deposited Roger's money and retrieved his change. Roger collapsed in laughter.

'What's so funny?'

'Do you get danger money for using that till?'

'I ought to.'

'Well if that draw hits your breasts, the rebound could destroy the till and the wall behind it!'

'Never mind the till,' Mandy replied 'What about my—' The phone behind the bar interrupted her. 'Sorry, Roger I have to get that.'

Roger went back to the table. 'OK George, all arranged. Dave will bring them over.'

In the background, Mandy's indistinct voice could be heard. 'I'm sorry Mrs Hunt, but Mike left here ages ago.'

Mandy put the phone down and walked into the bar area and started shouting. 'Has anybody seen Mike Hunt?'

'Did she just say what I thought she said?' asked Guy 'Has anyone seen her what???'

Mandy moved around the bar shouting 'Has anybody seen Mike Hunt?'

People were starting to laugh and whisper to each other.

Mandy came to the table. 'Have any of you guys seen Mike Hunt?'

'I have,' said several voices in unison.

'I'd love to,' said Guy.

'I'm hoping to later on!' said Roger.

'Oh come on guys, don't mess about,' said Mandy 'Have you seen him? That was his wife on the phone, very worried because he hasn't arrived home. He left here ages ago.'

'Perhaps he's got another woman?' suggested George.

'Really, George?' replied Mandy 'you know Mike. Forever tapping his wedding ring and saying 'happily married man' and 'promised to another'.'

'True. He'll turn up' said George after some thought.

Mandy sidled round to Roger. 'Roger, you flew with him today, did he seem OK to you?'

'Well, it was the first time I had met him, so I wouldn't know,' said Roger 'he sounded like a trainspotter but otherwise OK.'

Roger pulled on Mandy's arm so that he could whisper in her ear. 'Anyway, when do you finish your shift?'

'Not for an hour or so,' she replied, 'Why?'

'Well, when you finish, why don't you come over and sit on my knee. We can talk about the first thing that pops up.'

Mandy smiled at him. 'Oh, you are forward, aren't you. OK, I see you in a while.'

Mandy walked back to the bar.

'I see you are taking my advice' piped up George.

'Why's that?' asked Roger.

George smiled. 'Well, what was all that whispering about?'

'Oh, I was asking her something about my invoice' lied Roger.

'Well, watch out, here comes your answer,' said George, who had spotted Mandy returning from the bar.

'Oh, no seats,' said Mandy, pretending to be surprised.

'Well, you're welcome to come and sit on my lap' offered Roger.

Mandy sat on Roger's lap but started to wiggle about. 'Ooh I'm not at all comfortable on your lap, it's awfully lumpy.'

Roger whispered in her ear. 'I thought you said you didn't finish for an hour?'

'I did, but we're not busy tonight, so Dave is quite happy to manage on his own,' she whispered back 'Look, it's not a good idea to be seen to leave together. I'll make an excuse to leave, give it a while before you leave, and I'll see you outside.'

Mandy stood up and yawned loudly. 'Well, I'll be off now. I must go and feed my cat.'

'I've been meaning to ask you, Mandy,' said Guy 'Does your pussy have whiskers?'

Mandy looked startled. 'I beg your pardon, Guy?'

'It's a simple question, Mandy. Does your pussy have whiskers?' he repeated.

Mandy stared at him, not knowing what to say.

'Or does it have some other kind of cat food?'

'Thank you, Guy,' said Mandy, clearly relieved, 'don't give up the day job. Bye, all.'

Roger tried to join back in the conversation, but he couldn't show much interest. Something better was waiting outside.

He yawned. 'Yes, it's been a long day. First flying lesson and all that. I think I'll go as well.'

He stood up. The whole table dissolved into laughter.

'What's so funny?' he asked.

'Nothing at all, Roger. You go and have a wonderful time with Mandy.'

'Well, it's been really nice to meet you all,' said Roger 'see you all next time.'

CHAPTER EIGHT

Roger stepped outside the club as darkness was falling.

'Hello, big boy!' He jumped as Mandy had grabbed him from behind.

'Hello, Mandy. My car is over there.'

Mandy held up some keys and rattled them. 'Oh, I think I can do better. These are the keys to the executive jet over there. Much more comfortable!'

Mandy led Roger over to the aircraft. She unlocked the door, let some stairs down, and they climbed inside and shut the door.

Mandy grabbed Roger and kissed him. Roger let his hands slide down her back and felt her bum. *Yes, she's definitely got a spanner bum* he thought.

Something moved inside his trousers.
Mandy felt the movement too. She undid his
zip and slid her hand inside.

'Oh,' Mandy was disappointed.

'Don't worry' whispered Roger 'have you
ever seen University Challenge?'

'Of course.'

'Well, that's your starter for ten.'

Mandy giggled. 'Now that's the sort of
challenge I like. Come on, the floor is far
more comfortable. Let's not waste this plush
carpet.'

CHAPTER NINE

Roger and Mandy emerged from the aircraft. Mandy locked the door, and they walked back towards the club. Suddenly they could hear faint cries for help.

Roger strained his ears. 'Listen, what's that noise?'

'Sounds like someone is in trouble and it seems to be coming from over there.'

They walked in the direction of the cries. In the half-light, they could see a strange-looking vehicle parked in front of a wall.

'What on earth is that?'

'Looks like an alien spacecraft. This could be Linton's answer to the Roswell Incident.'

As they got closer, they saw a strange glow and a figure moving about inside.

'Whatever it is, it's not dead yet,' said Roger.

Then a frantic face suddenly appeared at the window.

'Good Lord, it's Mike,' said Mandy.

'Help, get me out of here!!' came Michael's muffled cries.

Roger walked around the vehicle 'Where's the door?'

'The door is at the front,' shouted Michael 'You'll need to push the car back.'

Roger and Mandy pushed the car back and opened up the whole front of the car.

A frantic Michael emerged. 'I've been stuck here for ages.'

'What happened?' asked Roger.

'That bloody Forsythe man is what happened. He's the accountant that wants to buy Jed's bar. Him and his flashy car, he ran me off the road. Just managed to stop before I hit the wall.'

Roger was puzzled. 'Why didn't you just reverse away from the wall?'

'This is an Isetta Bubble car. It's got no reverse gear. It's a three-wheeler; well actually it's a bloody motor-bike!'

'That explains it. When I first saw it, I thought it might be some type of alien spacecraft.'

'Anyway, thank you both for your assistance, but I must away. My wife will be wondering where I am.'

'Yes, your wife rang in earlier. We told her you had left ages ago.'

Michael climbed back into his vehicle. 'Thank you both. Goodnight.' He closed the front and drove away.

'Imagine,' said Roger 'if you lived alone, had an automatically closing garage door and accidentally parked too close to the end of the garage, it could be years before your body was found.'

'Indeed,' agreed Mandy 'who needs Dignitas when you've got one of those things.'

Roger turned to Mandy 'Well, thanks for a very enjoyable evening. I'd better be--'

'Oh, does it need to end now?' interrupted Mandy sadly.

She dangled the keys in front of his face. 'I've still got the keys, and I've still got the inclination if you have?'

'Oh, I think so. Come on then, Spanner-bum.'

'Spanner-bum? Why do you call me that?'

'Because it tightens my nuts up every time I see it!'

They walked back to the aircraft, climbed in and shut the door.

'Ooh, you remind me of Jesus,' said Mandy 'I love a man that can rise again.'

'Hasn't taken me three days though, has it?' replied Roger.

CHAPTER TEN

Roger was asleep in bed next to his wife, Alison. She poked him in the ribs. 'Wake up, Roger!'

Roger opened his eyes and blinked, 'What's the matter?'

'You are the matter, Roger,' said Alison 'what time did you get in last night?'

'Oh, I'm not sure,' mumbled Roger 'About ten-thirty?'

'No, it wasn't. It was half-past midnight.'

'Well if you're already sure what time it was, why bloody well ask? And why didn't you say something when I came to bed?'

'Because I guessed you would have been drinking and I know what you get like when you have been drinking.'

'What, wanting sex with my wife you mean?'

'Well, you know what I think about that!'

'Huh! Don't I just.'

'So where were you until after midnight?'

'I went to the Linton Flying Club. Nice people. I had a trial lesson, and then they recommended I join the flying club bar. I met some other pilots there, and one thing led to another.' Roger smiled to himself 'It was a very enjoyable evening.'

'Oh, tell me you are not still thinking of trying to learn to fly are you after all I've said?'

Roger got out of bed 'Yes, I am. I really enjoyed my trial lesson yesterday.' He walked to a table. 'Look, they have given me a log-book to log my hours in and this book "Learning to fly" which explains what you have to do to become a pilot. You have to have 45 hours of flying training plus ground school training including air law, meteorology and navigation. I've got another lesson booked for later today.'

'Oh, give it up now, Roger. Another of your silly ideas. Far too expensive, and we need the money for the extension.'

'My Dad left me that money for me to realise my lifelong ambition. I'm not going to squander it starting a coven for your Mother. Before long she'll have two friends round, and they'll be casting for a production of Macbeth.'

'Oh, you do talk some rubbish, Roger. Anyway you are up now, so are you going in the bathroom first?'

'Yes.'

'Well, don't take all day. I'm much quicker than you are.'

'Yes dear, but you don't have to shave' he paused briefly 'every day!'

'Oh, funny Roger. You can always make me laugh, particularly every time you take your pants off!'

'Oh, you have the bloody bathroom first. I need a cup of tea.'

Roger left the room. Alison got out of bed, walked to the table and looked at the books. She picked up a pen and scribbled something across the front of one of them.

CHAPTER ELEVEN

Roger and Alison were eating breakfast.

'Now don't forget that you are coming with me to visit Mother tomorrow, will you?'

'Oh no, not again? We only saw her last week.'

'Now Roger, you know perfectly well that was four weeks ago.'

'Was it? Well, it only seems like last week. The trauma seems to last longer each time.'

'Don't be silly, Roger. Mother quite likes you.'

'Does she? I dread to think what she would be like if she didn't.'

'Anyway, don't forget. Tomorrow morning. No excuses.'

Roger made a loud groan, got up and went into the toilet. After a few moments, loud sniffing noises could be heard. Alison looked puzzled, got up and opened the toilet door. Roger was on his knees with his head down the toilet.

'Now come on, Roger. Don't tell me you are going to pretend to be sick, so you don't have to visit Mother?'

Roger got up. 'No, I was just getting used to the smell of piss!'

'Roger!! Oh, you are impossible. I'm going to work.'

Alison stormed out of the house and slammed the door. BANG!

Roger breathed a sigh of relief, got his coat but stopped before leaving.

Ah, I nearly forgot my books! He thought.

He went upstairs.

Roger walked to the table. He picked up his books and saw what Alison had scribbled on the front of "Learning to fly".

'AND PIGS MIGHT FLY,' he read out loud 'The cow!'

He collected his books together and left the house.

CHAPTER TWELVE

Roger entered Flight Training reception. Mandy was behind the desk.

'Hi Mandy, I've got a lesson booked with Mike.'

'Hello, Roger. He's about to finish with another student, so he won't be long. Take a seat, plenty of flying magazines to read while you wait.'

Roger sat down and picked up a magazine.

'While no one else is around Roger,' said Mandy 'I just wanted to say how much I enjoyed last night.'

Roger smiled at her. 'So did I.'

Mandy smiled back. 'You didn't say, but I suppose you are married?'

'Yes, I am.'

'Any kids?'

'No. None. Not likely to with my wife's attitude to sex. Mind you, she did warn me. When I first met her, she showed me her school report and on the front of it, it said 'Name, Alison Brown', 'Sex, F'. Not much of a grade, I thought. But being an optimistic sort of chap I thought never mind, maybe with a bit of practise we can get that up to an A or even an A+. But it wasn't to be. Anyway, I hear you are married as well?'

The door opened, and a man walked into reception.

'Yes, I am. Same problem I'm afraid.' She turned to the man 'Hello Mr Hamilton, what can I do for you?'

'Ah, Mandy. I need an engineer to check my executive jet. I've just been in it, and I found a damp patch on the carpet.'

Roger looked up from his magazine. Mandy went white.

'I'm not sure if I've got a leak in the roof or a hydraulic pipe is cracked. But I better not fly it until it's been checked. Can you arrange that, please? I think you've got a spare key here, haven't you?'

'Err, yes I'm sure we have Mr Hamilton.'

'Are you OK, Mandy?' asked Mr Hamilton 'You look like you've seen a ghost.'

'Yes, I'm fine, thank you, Mr Hamilton,' said Mandy 'Don't worry, I'll ring you when I have the result.'

'Thank you, Mandy,' said Mr Hamilton as he walked out the door.

Roger and Mandy stare at each other in horror and then burst into laughter.

'Oh God, I thought I was going to die when he complained about the damp carpet!' said Mandy.

'Me too!' replied Roger 'Didn't know where to put myself.'

The door to Michael Hunt's office opened, and Michael and a pupil emerged.

'Well, goodbye, Mr Golding,' said Michael 'Be sure to read up on your air law, as you need to pass that exam before I can send you solo.'

Mr Golding nodded and left the building.

'Ah, hello again, Mr Moore,' said Michael 'Are you ready for another lesson?'

'Oh, absolutely, Michael' said Roger 'I can't wait.'

'That's the spirit, Mr Moore, that's the spirit,' said Michael enthusiastically 'Mandy, could you book us out in Hotel-Tango please?'

'I can, Mike,' replied Mandy 'but I think you should be aware that the last pilot to fly it said the press-to-talk button on the pilot's side was a bit iffy. Kept sticking.'

'OK Mandy, thank you, we'll keep an eye on it,' said Michael 'Come on, Mr Moore, your aircraft awaits.'

CHAPTER THIRTEEN

'Well Mr Moore, you've grasped flying straight and level, climbing, descending and turning,' said Michael, 'Time to re-join the circuit I think. Give Air Traffic a call.'

'What me?' asked Roger with a note of trepidation in his voice.

'Yes, Mr Moore. You. You'll need to talk to them sooner or later. They won't bite. Press the button on the control column and say Linton Tower, Hotel- Tango for re-join. Then read their answer back to them and add Hotel-Tango at the end. Go on.'

Roger gingerly pressed the PTT button.

'Err Linton Tower, Hotel-Tango for re-join.'

'Roger Hotel-Tango. Hold position, you are number two in traffic. I'll call you back shortly.'

Feeling nervous about the unexpected message, Roger pressed the PTT button too hard.

'Hold position, number two in traffic, Hotel-Tango.'

Roger released the button, but it stuck, and the radio stayed on transmit.

The Air Traffic Controllers in Linton Tower listened in horror as the conversation coming from Hotel-Tango continued to be received on their radio.

'Excellent, Mr Moore. Your first contact with ATC. We must stay around here until they give us permission to proceed. So while we are waiting, let me thank you again for coming to my assistance last night.'

'No problem. I'm glad we did as you could still be there. Never mind Dignitas in Switzerland, they should sell those bubble cars as a do-it-yourself suicide kit!'

'The bloody PTT switch on Hotel-Tango has stuck again,' said one controller to another 'I'll get the other aircraft to change frequency.'

He picked up the microphone. 'Linton Tower broadcast. All aircraft on this frequency, to avoid interference, please call Linton Approach on One Three Two decimal One Five.'

He turned to the other controller. 'Can you deal with the other aircraft when they call in on that frequency? I'll stick with Hotel-Tango until they realise what's happened.'

In Hotel-Tango, Michael and Roger continued their conversation.

'I suppose it's a stupid question, but why were you there with Mandy?'

'Ah, well, as you say. Stupid question.'

Roger continued with some passion. 'It seems we both suffer from the same problem when it comes to sex. Disinterested partners. Before I met Mandy, I was seriously considering joining a bloody monastery. I've always loved sex and I've always been a great admirer of the female form. All those curves and lumps and bumps. I mean before sex, the vagina looks like a jewel in a velvet case.' He thought for a moment, 'Mind you, afterwards it can look more like a nasty road accident!'

'Yes, yes, Mr Moore, please spare me the lurid details,' said Michael. 'Let us just say

you succumbed to her womanly charms.
Now, what's happened to ATC, have they
forgotten us? Although I haven't noticed
them talk to any other aircraft either.' He
pressed his PTT button. 'Linton Tower,
Hotel-Tango.'

In Linton Tower, the controller answered,
'Go ahead, Hotel-Tango.'

'Nothing heard. Strange. Oh! Maybe that
bloody button has stuck again. Quick, click
the button on your control column.'

Roger frantically clicked his PTT button,
and suddenly there was Linton Tower.

'Thank you, Hotel-Tango for that
entertaining interlude. Please don't fly
Hotel-Tango again until the faulty PTT
switch has been replaced. Cleared to land
runway Two Six, QFE Niner Niner Four.
Wind calm.'

'Cleared to land runway Two Six. Niner
Niner Four. Please accept my apologies.'

'Apologies accepted Mike.' In the Tower,
the two controllers dissolved into laughter.

'We'd better run a recording of that
conversation off pronto and send it to the
boys. That'll be worth more than a few pints
in the flying club bar!!'

CHAPTER FOURTEEN

Michael and Roger walked back into reception.

'I'd keep quiet about that incident if I were you,' whispered Michael to Roger, 'We don't really want anyone to know what happened. Doesn't show the club in a favourable light.' Roger nodded.

'A satisfactory lesson completed today, Mr Moore. Well done!.'

'Thanks, Michael.'

'Oh Mandy, can you ground Hotel-Tango and book an engineer to replace the pilot side PTT switch, please. It definitely is faulty.'

'OK Mike, will do,' replied Mandy.

Michael disappeared back into his office.

Roger turned to Mandy. 'So I'm going over to the club bar now. What are you doing later?'

'Oh, I'm sorry, Roger, I must go home after I finish here. Hubby is getting suspicious. He noticed I had my knickers on back to front and inside out when I got home last night.'

'Oh, that's a shame. Another time perhaps' said Roger.

'Absolutely, Roger.'

CHAPTER FIFTEEN

Roger walked to the bar. Dave was serving.

'Hello, Roger. What would you like to drink?'

'A pint of bitter please.'

Roger looked around the bar while Dave poured him a pint. He noticed everyone seemed to be listening to their mobile phones and laughing. He spotted Guy sitting at a table on his own and decided to join him.

'Hello, Guy. Remember me from last night?'

'Oh, indeed I do,' replied Guy in a Prince Charles voice, 'How could one forget? You went off with Randy Mandy. Did one observe a jewel in a velvet case?'

Roger was startled. 'Err what???'

'And one really, really hopes the jewel in a velvet case ended up looking like a nasty road accident.'

'Guy, what are you on about?'

'Come on Roger, don't be coy. We've all listened to the recording. Air Traffic sent it around the club.'

'On no, how could they? The bloody button stuck at the worst possible moment.'

'Oh, don't worry,' said Guy reassuringly, 'All part of the fun and banter of the club. Expect to be teased for a while, but at least everyone now knows who you are. You lived up to your name, you certainly have rogered more!'

'Yes, I'm sure you will all be taking the piss. Incidentally, where is everyone? A much bigger crowd here yesterday.'

'Oh, they'll all be in when they can. They all have home lives, jobs etc.'

'I suppose so,' said Roger, looking around, 'So where do you do the disco? This room doesn't seem big enough.'

'Far too small,' agreed Guy, 'See the wooden partition wall over there? Behind, there is a larger room with a small stage. It's where it all happens.'

'So what do you do apart from discos? Do you have another job?'

'Yes. I serve food and drink to the mentally sub-normal, alcoholics, down and outs and the like.'

'Eminently commendable, Guy. So who do you work for, social services or a charity perhaps?'

'No, no. I work at Wetherspoons,' said Guy. 'See the chap being served at the bar? His name is Malcolm. He's one of the Air Traffic guys responsible for the recording. Oh, he's coming over.'

'Hello Guy,' said Malcolm 'did you receive the recording?'

'Yes, I did. Brilliant wasn't it?' replied Guy, 'Oh Malcolm, this is Roger. Roger, this is Malcolm, he's an Air Traffic Controller.'

'I'm pleased to meet you, Malcolm.'

'Likewise, Roger. Are you sure we haven't met before? Your voice seems awfully familiar.'

'It bloody well should be, Malcolm. You sent me a recording of it!'

Malcolm couldn't hide his embarrassment. 'Oh shit! Sorry Roger, but we always send stuff like that around the members. Nothing personal. Look on the bright side, you've entered the Linton Flying Club Hall of Fame!'

'Yes, that's what Guy said. I'm not sure if I'll be famous or infamous. I only started lessons yesterday. So how long have you been an Air Traffic Controller?'

'Oh, about five years now. The pay isn't bad, the work isn't that hard, and occasionally a stuck PTT button brightens our day up.'

'So what does an Air Traffic Controller's job entail?'

'Well, there are about five hundred million cubic miles of flyable airspace in the world. The chances of two aircraft hitting each other are next to zero. Zilch. So to justify our existence, we insist that aircraft fly down five-mile wide invisible corridors in the sky so that we, Air Traffic Control, need to be there to keep them from hitting each other, and hey presto, I have a job for life.'

'Where does the money come from to pay your wages?'

'Landing fees. You can take off as many times as you like, we only charge you for the landings!'

Roger looked puzzled. 'But?'

'Don't look so puzzled Roger, the last part was a joke.'

'Oh, right.'

'Here, we only control the airfield itself and the immediately surrounding airspace. If Air Traffic tells you the runway is clear, then you may enter. Unless you are at Tenerife North airport when you ask are you sure?'

Roger looked puzzled again. 'Sorry I--?'

'A cardinal rule is only one aircraft is allowed on a runway at a time,' Malcolm continued 'At Tenerife North airport, due to fog, two Boeing 747s collided on the runway. The world's worst air disaster ever. Five hundred and eighty-three people killed. All pilots, crew and passengers. Luckily for the air traffic controller, at the subsequent enquiry, he was the only one involved that was actually there.'

'Oh, how awful.'

'It was. So always do what Air Traffic tells you. We are usually right, but obviously not always!'

'I'll bear that in mind. So do you only work in the day?'

'No, the airfield is open 24/7. Though why anyone would want to fly a light aircraft at night, I can't imagine. Not sure about in the day either. Birds and Turds fly by day, Bats and Twats at night. I think I'll keep my feet on terra-firma, thank you. Anyway, I'm pleased to have met the voice in the flesh, so to speak. I'll catch you guys later.'

CHAPTER SIXTEEN

Malcolm walked out of the bar as three people walked in, laughing and listening to a mobile phone.

George spotted Roger and put his phone away, hushing the other two. 'Hello, Roger, nice to meet you again.'

'Likewise, George. Something amusing on your phone?'

'Oh, so you know about that, do you? I was trying to spare your blushes. Mind if we join you?'

They all sat down.

'Right. Introductions. Roger, this is Keith and Steve. Keith, Steve, this is Roger.'

'Hi, Roger,' said Steve.

'Not the Roger we've been listening to?' asked Keith.

'Yes, that's me, Keith. Joke of the week.'

'No, no, no. A jewel in a velvet case and a nasty road accident,' said Keith 'When I first heard it, it was a jewel in a velvet case before, and a bulldog eating mayonnaise after. Anyway, you were so descriptive. You are quite the linguist Roger, and a cunning one at that I'd say, for you to notice such things!'

'So are you a pilot, Keith?'

'Yes. I'm an instructor, and I'm hoping to go commercial shortly. You might be lumbered with me if Mike is ill or gets permanently incarcerated in that bloody bubble car thing of his.'

'Yes, the thing is a death trap,' agreed Roger 'I had to help him out of it last night. He said that the accountant that wants to buy Jed's bar, Forsythe I think his name is, had run him off the road with his Roller. He sounds a nasty piece of work.'

'Yes he is,' said George 'He put all the Flight Training prices up when he took that over. Typical accountant, he knows the price of everything and the value of nothing. Accountants should be limited by law to only doing other peoples books! If he gets his grubby paws on this place, then that will be the end of it, and that will be a tragedy. Take a glance around, airline crews, pilots, air traffic controllers, ground crews, customs etc all enjoying themselves. What a wonderful environment. Jed has done a great job keeping it this way.'

'So Steve, are you are a pilot as well?' asked Roger.

'Yes, I qualified here about three years ago,' replied Steve, 'but it was before Forsythe got his sweaty palms on the place. Couldn't afford to do it now. Had enough trouble as it was. I work for BT, so I managed to add a bit to my wages by doing hooky wiring and extension phones in my spare time. Anyway, excuse me a moment, nature calls.'

George looked round. 'Where is Steve going?'

'Call of nature, he said.'

'Is it bollocks! It's his bloody round. The tight-fisted git always disappears when it's his round.'

'Well, never mind. I'll buy the round.'

Roger went to the bar. 'Dave, can you organise a round of drinks for the table over there, please.'

Dave studied the table. 'OK, Roger, I think I know what everyone wants. I'll bring them over.'

'How the hell do you remember what everyone drinks?'

'Oh, just a knack. I've been a barman for a long time.'

'You are definitely the best barman I've ever come across.'

'Thanks, Roger. Make the most of it while you can.'

'What do you mean?'

'I can't tell you any more, I'm afraid. Just don't go for a while. Jed is going to make an announcement.'

Roger went back to the table. 'Dave is being very mysterious tonight. Says Jed is going to make an announcement.'

'What about?' asked George.

'He wouldn't say.'

'I'll see if I can find more out when he brings the drinks over,' said Guy.

Steve returned from the toilet and sat down.

'I thought you had a call of nature?' said George.

'I did,' said Steve.

'Took you a long while.'

'Well I had a bad curry last night, and I've just had a Captain Kirk moment.'

'What the hell is a Captain Kirk moment?' asked Roger.

'I had a lot of trouble with the Klingons,' replied Steve.

'It was your bloody round,' said George 'Why do you always disappear when you should be in the chair?'

'Oh, was it? Never mind, I'll get the next one.'

'I saw you peeping through the door, making sure someone else had gone to the bar.'

'No, I didn't.'

'Hey, guys, what's the difference between Steve and a coconut?'

'I don't know George, what is the difference between Steve and a coconut?' everybody shouted.

'You can get a bloody drink out of a coconut!'

They all laughed except Steve. Dave arrived with the drinks and handed them out.

'Where's mine?' asked Steve.

'You weren't at the table when Roger asked for the round' explained Dave.

'You'll have to buy your own bloody beer now. Serves you right,' said George.

'Never mind about Steve,' said Guy 'Dave, Roger says you are being mysterious. Something about an announcement?'

'I can't say any more,' said Dave 'Just hang around. Oh, here's Jed now.'

CHAPTER SEVENTEEN

Suddenly all the lights in the club came on.

'Ladies and Gentlemen,' shouted Jed.

He paused for the noise to abate.

'Ladies and Gentlemen. Please can I have your attention? Now as I'm sure you all know, a couple of years ago I sold the flight training side to Dave Forsythe--'

Jed stopped. The name Dave Forsythe caused an uproar from the crowd. They were shouting abuse.

'Bastard put all the prices up--'

'He's a rip off merchant--'

'Ladies and Gentlemen, please. When I sold it to David Forsythe, I agreed that within two years he had the option to buy the club bar as well.'

The uproar continued.

'No! Don't sell it to the bastard!'

'Last week, I decided to retire completely. David Forsythe is taking up that option as of midnight tonight, and will be the new owner of the flying club bar.'

Further abuse came from the crowd. Beer mats were thrown at Jed.

'He'll ruin the bloody place--'

'He'll turn the place into a disco or a night club--'

'So can I just thank you all for your custom and friendship these last few years. I wish you all every success with your flying and I that hope you continue to enjoy the facilities of this wonderful club. Thank you all and goodbye.'

Jed left the club. There was so much shouting that no one saw a shadowy figure watching the proceedings through a partially open door. He drew on a Big Cuban cigar, glanced at his watch, then turned and left the club. Outside, he took the cigar from his mouth, dropped it on the ground and trod on it. He took one step forward, paused, farted loudly then climbed into a Rolls Royce and drove away.

CHAPTER EIGHTEEN

Roger was sitting in the kitchen surrounded by books.

'Come on Roger, we'll be late,' said Alison.

'Alison, I've told you a hundred times, I don't want to go to your Mothers,' said Roger.

'Why on earth not?'

'I've got a lot of studying to do. Look at all these books. There's Air Law, Navigation, Meteorology. So much to learn'.

'I can't go to Mothers without you.'

'Why not? You've got your own car, you can drive, you are happy with the smell of piss.'

'If only you would speak to Mother, you might find you liked her.'

'Well, I don't like to interrupt her. But I do have a soft spot for her.'

'Really?'

'Yes, it's that bit of ground behind the garage where nothing will grow. You know that Mother-in-law is an anagram of Woman Hitler don't you?'

'Oh behave, Roger! What reason can I give Mother as to why you are not with me?'

'Well tell her anything, she won't remember it anyway. Tell her I'm learning to fly, tell her I'm dead.'

'Roger! How dare you say that? I can't tell her you are dead.'

'Why not? Probably please her. Then she can delete me from her spells and focus on some other poor bastard. Second thoughts though, don't tell her I'm learning to fly.'

'Why not?'

'I don't want to be at two thousand feet in a Cessna One Five Two and suddenly find myself in a formation with a witch on a broomstick!'

'Oh! Roger, you are completely impossible. I'm off to Mothers by myself. I'll tell her you've been sectioned because you were having delusions about learning to fly.'

Alison got up and stormed out of the house and slammed the door. BANG!

Roger breathed a sigh of relief. He looked at his book and read out loud.

'Air has weight, and density is simply the weight of the number of molecules of air present in a given volume of air. Not sure about that. Let me try something else. When a parcel of air gets heated, it expands and rises because it is now less dense than the surrounding air.'

He sighed and put his head in his hands.

Meteorology is more difficult than I thought. I'll take the book with me and pop into the club later on. Maybe I can get some help.

He grabbed his coat and left the house.

CHAPTER NINETEEN

Roger walked into reception.

Mandy was behind the counter. 'Hello, Roger.'

'Hello Mandy, how are things?'

'Not too good, Roger. Mike's been sacked.'

'Sacked? I thought he ran the place.'

'Well he did effectively,' explained Mandy 'But it's been owned by Forsythe for a couple of years now, but he left it to Mike to run it. We rarely saw him. But now he has the club bar as well, he has more reason to be about. You know he ran Mike off the road the other night, well he came in today, and Mike had a right go at him. Forsythe swore at him and sacked him on the spot. He's left me in charge today and said he's got a new Chief

Flying Instructor coming sometime tomorrow, a chap called Lewis Davidson.'

'Bit harsh to sack him. After all, he had a point being run off the road like that and having to wait to be rescued. If we hadn't come along, he could have been there all night. Could have died of hypothermia.'

'Yes. Seems Mr Forsythe is as bad as they say he is.'

'So how are things at home?'

'Much the same, Roger. He's not talking to me. Giving me the silent treatment. But what does he expect? Everybody has needs, and if they are not satisfied at home, then you are bound to look elsewhere. How about you?'

'Well Alison has no reason to suspect anything, she's just being her normal obnoxious self. Doesn't want me to learn to fly or more likely doesn't think I'm capable of doing it. Mind you, I am finding the ground school a bit difficult. Meteorology in particular. That's why I'm here today, hoping to find someone to help me. I should have gone with her to visit her mother, but I'm not keen on hedgehog pie for lunch and her Mother incessantly going on about why we haven't blessed her with any grandchildren yet.'

'Yes, that all sounds too familiar. But as far as help with Met goes, no one else is here. You might find someone in the club bar or perhaps wait until your next lesson.'

'So are you completely on your own?' asked Roger with a glint in his eye.

'Yes. Why?'

'I was just thinking you might have a stationery cupboard, or somewhere we could renew old acquaintances?'

'Oh Roger, I'd love to, but Forsythe has left me in a responsible position.'

'Um, that wasn't the sort of position I was thinking of.'

'No. If he came back and caught us he would sack me too, and I do need this job.'

'Point taken,' said Roger 'I'll take your advice, and hop over to the club bar and see if anyone can help me with my meteorology problems. Can you join me when you finish here?'

'Err well OK. Can't stay long though.'

'OK, I'll see you later.'

Roger gave Mandy a kiss and left reception.

CHAPTER TWENTY

Roger walked into the bar and stopped dead. The bar had changed. Furniture had been covered, ladders rested against walls and the smell of paint was overwhelming.

'What the??'

A slightly coarse female voice shouted. 'That bar is closed. Go round to the other side!'

Roger exited by the usual door and went round to the other bar. He was confronted by a rather obese 18yr old standing behind the bar, chewing gum.

'We're doing that bar up, so we are using this one. I'm Chantelle. What's ya poison?'

'Pint of bitter, please Chantelle.'

Chantelle picked up a pint glass and poured a pint but left a large head. Roger stared at the foam in dismay.

'I asked for a pint of bitter, not half a pint of froth.'

Chantelle gave Roger a dirty look but picked up the pint and managed to clear the foam. She slammed the glass on the bar. Roger picked it up and took a mouthful. He spluttered and spat it back into the glass.

'This beer's gone!'

Chantelle stared at him in disbelief.

'No, it bloody ain't! Someone else said that earlier on but I've bin into the cellar and shaken the barrel and there's plenty left in there!'

'That's not what gone means. Oh! bloody hell, is Dave around?'

'Dave who? There's no one 'ere but me.'

'Oh, never mind, I can't drink that crap. Give me a bottle instead.'

Chantelle picked up a bottle, took the top off and put it on the bar.

'Err, what am I going to drink it out of??'

'The bottle, of course.'

'I think I'm older than 20. I'll use a glass please.'

'OK Grandad, keep ya hair on!'

Chantelle put a glass on the bar. 'That'll be £8.'

Roger was upset. '£8? The bottles are usually £5.'

'Don't moan at me, Grandad. The man in the roller gave me this price list, and it says £8!'

Roger gave her £8. He looked around the bar and spotted Guy sitting next to the stage, sorting some records. He went over.

CHAPTER TWENTY-ONE

'Hello, Guy. So is this where all your music magic happens?'

'Hello, Roger. Yes, this is my little stage.'

'And you are still using vinyl? I thought you would store them all as MP3s on your phone and Bluetooth it straight into the amplifier.'

'No, no, you can't beat vinyl. The punters demand it.'

'After five pints, surely they wouldn't know any different? Talking of pints, who is that idiot serving behind the bar?'

'Oh, you've met dear Chantelle then. Not got much between her ears, has she? Bloody Forsythe, now he owns the place, he's only gone and sacked Dave. Apparently, Dave's expertise behind the bar was too expensive for him, so he's installed Chantelle. I imagine she is on minimum wage, then again she has got minimum brains.'

Roger looked up as several people entered the bar. They were all air-crew in uniform. They went to the bar led by the one with the most rings on his sleeve. He was older, authoritative and had a handlebar moustache.

'OK guys, who wants what? So one, two, three pints of bitter, and girls? G and Ts?, so one, two, three G and Ts.' He turned to Chantelle. 'Ah, young lady, three pints of bitter and three G and Ts please.'

Chantelle began to pull pints from the pump she had used earlier. Roger noticed and went over to the bar. 'I'm sorry to interrupt, but the beer in that pump has gone. I've tried it and it is disgusting.'

'Oh, thanks for letting us know. Young lady, I suggest you do the G and Ts and ask Dave to change the barrel.'

'Dave who?' asked Chantelle. 'Why does everyone keep going on about Dave? There ain't no Dave here, only me.'

'Oh dear, I'll go and find Jed.'

'I don't think that will be possible. Jed's gone. He's sold the bar to Forsythe,' said Roger.

'Oh my God, no! That explains everything. The painters in the other bar.' He looked at Chantelle. 'The cheap labour.'

'Oi, Walrus Face, who you calling cheap?'

'I don't suppose that muppet Forsythe is around is he?' asked Walrus Face.

'Don't think so. He gave me a price list, showed me how to use the till and then buggered off in his roller.'

Walrus Face sighed and turned to Roger. 'Sorry old chap, we haven't been introduced. I'm Captain Slack, James Slack and you are?'

'I'm Roger. Roger Moore.'

'Oh, any relation to--'

'No. None. I started to learn to fly yesterday.'

'Oh well done old chap. Excellent.'

Chantelle returned with three G and T's.

'The girls have their G and Ts,' said Roger 'I would recommend the bottled beer for you gents.'

'Indeed. Three bottles please, young lady. I say thanks for helping us out there, Roger. This place seems to have gone to the dogs already.'

Chantelle returned with three bottles.

'Can you provide some glasses for those beers please, young lady. Jake, your round, I think. Pay the girl.'

'So have you just been on a flight?' asked Roger.

'Yes, we flew out to Lanzarote early this morning and back this afternoon. This bar is a godsend to us crews. Whatever time we return, we can eat food and drink beer without leaving the airport. Wonderful,' He paused. 'Or at least it was.'

'So your crew, I suppose the men are all pilots, and the women are hostesses?'

'Good Lord, no. Not these days. The two men are stewards, and two of the women are pilots. First Officers to be precise. There are more and more women pilots coming through the ranks these days. It won't be long before we have to rename the bloody cockpit to the cu--'.

'Yes, yes,' interrupted Roger, 'I think I get your drift!'

Captain Slack took Roger's arm and moved to where the crew was standing.

'So let me introduce you to the crew. This is Sandy and Jennifer, they are first officers, this is Kyle and Jake, they are stewards, and

this young lady is Beverley, she's a hostess.
Crew, meet Roger Moore, he is just learning
to fly.'

'Hi Roger,' said Beverley.

'Roger Moore?' asked Sandy 'Is that your
name or your ambition?'

Roger smiled at her. 'That's been asked
before. Both actually.'

'Ooh get him,' said Kyle in a slightly
effeminate voice. 'Lothario or what?'

'So why just a steward Kyle?' asked Roger
'Would being a pilot be too exciting?'

'Oh no, sweet cheeks, I'm a people person,'
replied Kyle 'I like keeping the hoi-polloi in
order. That can be quite exciting as well you
know. I had one silly woman on a flight, I
asked her to put her tray up because we
were coming into land. Next time I walked
past, the tray is still down. So I asked her
again. She gazed up at me and said in a sexy
husky voice "In my country, I am a Princess,
so I do as I please". So I told her, "Look, love,
in my country, I am a Queen, so I outrank
you. So put the bloody tray up, bitch!".'

Roger laughed. 'Quite a funny story, Kyle.
Is it true?'

'Oh absolutely.'

'Oh yes, you wouldn't believe the fun we have with the passengers,' said Jake 'On one flight we were going through some quite severe turbulence and this woman was convinced she was going to die. She got quite hysterical and said, "before I die, I just want a real man to make me feel like a real woman one last time." Well if I do say so myself, I have quite a masculine physique--'

'Oh he does, he does' interrupted Kyle.

'--so I walked up to her, took my shirt off, rippled my muscles, looked her straight in the eye and said: "OK then, iron that!".'

Kyle and Jake dissolved into laughter.

'Definitely not true, that one,' said Roger.

'Oh no, but a funny story nonetheless.'

'So flying must be well-paid with all these people wanting to become pilots and stewards. Can flying make you a millionaire?' asked Roger.

Captain Slack laughed 'Oh yes, dear boy, it can. But only if you are a billionaire when you start out!'

Roger turned around and saw that Guy had been joined by others. 'Well, it's been great to meet you all. I must get back to my friends.'

'Lovely to meet you as well and thanks for helping out with the beer earlier,' said Captain Flack. 'I'm sure we'll be seeing more of you.'

'I hope so, Roger!' said Sandy with a wink.

CHAPTER TWENTY-TWO

Roger went back to where Guy was sitting. He had been joined by George and others.

'Hello Roger,' said George 'You've met Captain Slack and his merry crew then.'

'Yes, I went over to warn him the beer was foul and got into conversation.'

'Forsythe is an idiot leaving a young girl in charge of a busy bar when she's got little or no idea how to run one.'

'Even worse he's sacked, Michael Hunt!'

'What?? Why the hell would he do that? Who the hell is going to run the training side of things?'

'Well Mike had a go at him for running him off the road the other night, and Forsythe sacked him on the spot. He's left Mandy in charge today and apparently there will be a new CFI sometime tomorrow. A chap called Lewis Davidson.'

'Never heard of him. This place gets worse and worse. Strikes me Forsythe is trying to run this place on a shoestring to make more money. But he's got rid of Dave and Mike, the two people that made the businesses run smoothly and profitably. He's a total idiot!'

'So it seems. In fact, someone in here was joking the other night, that accountants should be restricted by law to only doing other people's books, and not allowed to run a business themselves. Not far wrong, eh?'

'That was me, Roger. Yes, they seem to know the price of everything and the value of nothing. Anyway, I was hoping to see you tonight, Roger. Steve and I have Oscar-November booked tomorrow for a flight to Le Touquet, and two passengers have let us down. So I thought you and your wife might like to join us. It will give you a feel for what you are aiming for in learning to fly and also give her a great day out, something she can do much more when you've got your own licence. We share the costs between us, and if you buy enough cheap fags and booze, it almost pays for itself. What do you say?'

'Well sounds great, and I would love to go, but I don't think Alison would come with me. She's probably not speaking to me at the minute as I didn't go with her to visit her mother, plus the fact she's not keen on me learning to fly.'

'Well I suppose you could always come on your own, but we prefer a plane full as it cuts down on the costs. Perhaps you can fill the other seat. We usually eat lunch at the airport restaurant; L'Escale is world-famous, then we walk into town in the afternoon. Le Touquet is a beautiful French coastal resort which used to be frequented by the Kings and Queens of England. Then we grab some booze and fags from one of the large supermarkets and fly back. It would be an excellent experience for you.'

'Sounds wonderful. I'll definitely come, and perhaps I can fill the other seat. I've got an idea.'

'OK, well be at reception at nine in the morning. Don't forget your passport. You shouldn't need it, but sometimes the frogs get a bit awkward. I'll show you how to fill in and file a flight plan and work out the route etc.'

'That would be so helpful, George. Thanks. Ah, here comes Mandy. Mandy, come here and sit down. Can I get you a drink?'

'Ah, what a gentleman. Pink gin please.'

Roger went to the bar where Chantelle was busy serving on her own. Eventually, she came over to Roger.

'Sorry about the wait,' she said.

Roger looked her up and down. 'Don't worry,' he said 'it'll come off if you exercise more.'

Chantelle was less than pleased at the remark. 'Are you looking for a knuckle sandwich, mate?'

'Sorry, just thinking out loud,' said Roger ' A pink gin please.'

Chantelle walked off and scrutinised the optics. Roger watched in amusement.

'Sorry mate, I've been all over the optics, and we ain't got any.'

'Yes, you have,' said Roger.

'I ain't. I've looked all over.'

'See the bottle of Angostura Bitters? Put two or three spots in a gin glass, swirl the glass around and tip it out into the sink. Then make a normal gin with ice and lemon. Now I wouldn't have had to explain that to Dave.'

'Dave, Dave, Dave, that's all I've heard all day. I think I'll change my bloody name!' Chantelle went off muttering.

'Having trouble with the hired help Roger?' Kyle appeared out of nowhere.

'Yes. I'm afraid Chantelle won't last very long behind this bar. We need a trained bar person. Got any more of your unlikely stories, Kyle?'

'Oh, loads love. Being a steward is a non-stop hoot. Passengers can be hilarious too. I said to one chap, 'would you like headphones?' And straight off he comes back "Oh yes please, Duckie, but how did you know my name was Phones?". Oh!, so bold!'

'Another of your stories, or was it true?'

'As true as I'm sitting here, love. Oh, here comes your drink. You don't look like a gin man to me.'

'I'm not. It's for the lady.'

'Really! And there's me thinking you had bought it for Mandy. Be lucky.'

'Thanks. See you around.'

'Not if I see you first, you won't!'

CHAPTER TWENTY-THREE

Roger gave Mandy the pink gin. 'There you go, girl. Now Mandy, how do you fancy an all-expenses-paid trip to France tomorrow?'

'What do you mean?' asked Mandy.

'Well, George and Steve have Oscar-November booked tomorrow to go to Le Touquet in France. George says it's a beautiful coastal resort, and the airport restaurant is world-famous. Two passengers have let them down, so they've offered me the first option to replace them. I'm dying to go, and it would make my day if you would come with me. What do you think?'

'Oh, I'm not sure, Roger. It sounds wonderful, but I'm really not sure. Why don't you take your wife?'

'Alison? She's probably got the hump with me at the minute. I don't think she would be interested. I'd much rather take you. You would enjoy it whereas she would be looking for something to moan about at every turn.'

'Oh, I'm still not sure, Roger. Tomorrow is my day off, but I've got stuff to do around the house and...'

'Well, there you are. No contest. What would you rather be doing, housework or going on a day-trip with a sexy, handsome chap in an aeroplane to where the Kings and Queens of England used to holiday?'

'Oh, so a sexy, handsome chap is coming as well? Why didn't you say earlier? You can definitely count me in!'

'No, handsome and sexy, I meant me!'

'I know that, Roger. I was just getting my own back for the two Mandys thing the other day. Yes, count me in, it sounds like a lot of fun, and I've seen from the met reports that tomorrow is going to be a lovely day both here and in northern France. Shall I bring my bathing cossy?'

'Not necessary, I hear there are lots of nudist beaches on the coast which visitors can use. Better bring your passport though.'

'Nudist beaches? No! Do you know what women my age have between their breasts which younger women don't?'

'No? What?'

'Their belly buttons, Roger. No way would I go nude in public at my age. Now, what time should I be here in the morning?'

'George said to be here at nine. Would that be a problem?'

'No, I don't think so. Hubby has to be at work at eight, so he'll be long gone. What time will we be back though, that could be a problem.'

'I've no idea.' Roger turned to George. 'George, Mandy is filling the last seat for tomorrow, but I was wondering what time we will be back?'

'Well we normally leave there about five, so we should be back here six-ish.'

'I suppose that will be OK. When I'm working, I often don't leave here until seven or sometimes later.'

'We usually have a couple of pints in here when we get back then retire to the local Chinky restaurant. Sometimes we bring back live crabs and lobsters, and Ken and Susie Wong make some amazing dishes for us.'

'Sounds delicious but I think I'll have to go straight home once we're back.'

'That would be such a shame if you did. George, who else is going tomorrow?'

'Well, it's myself and Steve, you and Mandy plus Guy and Bob.'

'I don't think I've met Bob yet.'

'Oh well, there's a treat in store for you. I've seen three black eyes in this club and Bob has had all three of them.'

'Oh dear, he sounds awful.'

'Well only when he's very drunk. He will be fine tomorrow, but he might pick you up on your French pronunciation though. He's a bit of a stickler for that.'

'I need to go, Roger. I'll be here at nine in the morning.'

'OK, well I'll walk you to your car.'

'Bye, all.'

'Bye'

'Don't be late.'

They walked to Mandy's car.

'Well, I'll hope we'll have a fun day out.'

'I hope so too. You are such a kind man, Roger. Your wife is lucky to have you. Come here.'

Mandy pulled him towards her and kissed him.

'Must go now.'
'OK. Bye.'

CHAPTER TWENTY-FOUR

Roger and Alison were eating breakfast. Roger was studying a book.

'You are not forgiven for yesterday, Roger.'

'Uh-huh.'

'For not coming with me to Mother's.'

'Uh-huh.'

'Roger! You are ignoring me.'

'Yes, I am. I'm studying.'

'Oh, you're not still on this flying thing are you?'

'Yes, I am. It is difficult I admit, but I'm determined to do it. I'm off to France today with some qualified pilots to get some proper flying experience.'

'France? Am I coming too?'

'You?? Of course not. You are not interested in me learning to fly.'

'Well, I wouldn't mind a day out in France. Where are you going?'

'Le Touquet.'

'Le Touquet! Yes! I've always wanted to go to L'Escale, the airport restaurant at Le Touquet. L'Escale is world-famous for its cuisine. The resort is lovely as well. The Kings and Queens--'

'--of England used to frequent it. Yes, I know. No, you can't come, there's only one spare seat. I only got invited because someone dropped out, and I was lucky enough to be around at the time.'

'Well perhaps someone else will drop out. I could come with you just in case? You speak so highly of the people at the club, I'd like to meet them.'

Roger turned white. 'Up until now anything to do with flying has been "verboten". Suddenly, when you spot a chance to fly to France, your attitude changes. Isn't that somewhat hypocritical?'

'Well, Susan at work went to L'Escale last year when they spent their holiday in France, and she said how wonderful it was.'

'Oh, right. You want to keep up with the Joneses. Well, I'm sorry, there is only one seat spare. When I'm qualified, we can fly to Le Touquet, Gibraltar, Malta or anywhere else in Europe. So perhaps you will be more encouraging with my flying in the future. Anyway, I must go, or I shall be late.'

Roger grabbed his coat and quickly headed for the door.

CHAPTER TWENTY-FIVE

Roger walked into reception. 'Morning all. Not late, am I?'

'No. I think we were all early, Roger' said George 'Now, you've met everyone but Bob, I think. Roger, this is Bob. Bob, this is Roger.'

'Hello, Bob. Pleased to meet you.'

'Likewise, Roger.'

'Now, the paperwork is done, Roger,' said George 'Come over here and I'll run through it with you.'

'OK, thanks, George.'

Roger winked at Mandy as George took him to a briefing area with maps on the wall and large books on a shelf.

'First, the weather. As you can see from this chart, an area of high pressure is covering most of the UK and northern

France. So few clouds and generally fine weather. OK so far?'

'Yes, that makes sense from what meteorology I have read,' agreed Roger.

'OK. So we need to let customs know where we are going, that is on a General Declaration or Gen Dec. Take a look, it's self-explanatory. Aircraft registration, the number of crew and passengers blah blah. Don't forget we need to give them one for the return flight. Now we need to fill in a flight plan as we are crossing the UK Flight Information Region border, we are going to France. Here is the form, you can see I've filled it out already. A bit more complicated, so we leave that for next time. Right if you come with me, we'll go to the tower and file these.'

'OK, that's a lot to remember, but I've got a general idea.'

'OK folks, Roger and I will file these in the tower, then we'll be off. If you all walk out to the plane, we'll be with you in five minutes.'

CHAPTER TWENTY-SIX

George and Roger walked into the tower. Malcolm was on duty.

'Hello, Malcolm.'

'Hello, George, and hello, Roger. Flying somewhere?'

'Le Touquet. Can we leave this flight plan with you?'

'Of course, you can. I'll put it in the system. Enjoy your trip and oh, Roger.'

'Yes?'

'Be careful with the PTT switch!'

'Yes, thank you for reminding me, Malcolm.'

'Anytime, Roger!'

'Right, now down to Customs,' said George.

They walked back down the stairs and into the Customs and Excise office.

'Hello Hugh, we've got some Gen Decs for you.'

'Hello George, where is it today? Jersey or Guernsey?'

'Neither Clever Clogs. Le Touquet.'

'Oh well, a change is as good as a rest, I suppose. Now don't bring back too much booze or too many fags. Personal use only remember.'

'You'd be surprised how much booze I can drink, and how many fags the wife can smoke!'

Hugh smiled. 'I'm sure I would, George. Have a nice day now.'

'Bye, Hugh.'

George and Roger emerged from the tower building and walked towards the aircraft.

'I'm amazed how friendly everyone is, particularly that customs guy,' said Roger.

'Oh, Hugh? You'll meet him in the bar at some point. He's fine. Now if we were going to the Channel Isles, then we would have had to go and see Special Branch as well.'

'Ah, they are scarier, are they?'

'No, not at all. Last time we went in there, they all laughed out loud and said 'Oh no, not you lot again. Give us that paperwork and F off! We're fed up with seeing you!' Not scary at all.'

'OK everybody, into the aircraft, and we'll be away.'

CHAPTER TWENTY-SEVEN

In the spectator's car park at Linton Airfield, two cars were parked, each with a person standing next to it. One man and one woman, taking a great interest in the people getting into the aircraft.

'The cow!' said the man.

'The bastard!' said the woman.

They turned and looked at each other.

'Problem?' asked the woman.

'Oh, sorry, I was thinking out loud.'

'I gathered that. I wondered why?'

'Well, my wife just got on that aircraft. She works at the club and today was her day off, but she told me she had to work. I was suspicious, so I thought I would come and see what she was up to. I'm glad I did. What was your interest in the aircraft?'

'Very similar, I suppose. My husband was on the aircraft as well. He has been having flying lessons at the club, but I got the feeling there was another attraction here as well. But it wouldn't be unusual for someone to have to work on their day off, would it? What made you so suspicious you decided to spy on her?'

'Oh well it's a bit embarrassing, and I've only just met you. Oh, what the hell, a few nights ago she got in late, and she had her underwear on back to front and inside out. The sort of thing that might happen if you had to put them back on in the dark.'

'The other night you say, funny that, my husband got in late a few nights ago after being here at the club. Interesting, I think we have a prima-facie case building here. I'm Alison, and you are?'

'I'm Dan'

'Pleased to meet you, Dan. Would you care to discuss it further over a cup of coffee?'

'Yes, I would. I know an excellent coffee bar in town. Follow me.'

They both got into their cars and drove off, just as Oscar-November left the runway and thundered overhead.

CHAPTER TWENTY-EIGHT

Oscar-November was over the English channel.

'Oh, what a fantastic view. Dover behind us, and I can just make out the French coast ahead,' remarked Mandy.

'Have you not been to Le Touquet before?' asked Roger in surprise.

'I've never been anywhere before, well not in a light aircraft.'

'Hang on, you mean that in all the time you've worked at the club and all the things you've done with, err I mean done for the members, no one has actually taken you on a trip with them before?'

'No, never. You're the first, Roger.'

'Well, what a bunch of mean, nasty bastards. I can't believe it. That's awful. I'm gob-smacked.'

The radio crackled into life. 'Oscar-November, London Information. Traffic information, in your eleven O'clock, three miles, left to right, a Cessna Two-Ten, five hundred feet above.'

'Oscar-November, can you be more explicit, please? We've all got digital watches these days' joked George.

'Very funny, Oscar-November. Don't worry, that traffic is clear of you now. Call Le Touquet Tower on One One Eight Decimal Four Five.'

'One One Eight Decimal Four Five. Oscar-November. Bye.'

'Enemy coast ahead Skipper,' piped up Steve.

'Le Touquet Tower, Oscar-November inbound to you from Linton.'

''ello Oscar-November. Cleared to finals number one, runway One Three, QNH One Zero One Five.'

'Cleared to finals number one, runway One Three, QNH One Zero One Five. Oscar-November.'

CHAPTER TWENTY-NINE

The aircraft taxied to a halt, and the propeller stopped turning.

Mandy stepped out on to the tarmac. 'Wow, what a lovely day. It's so hot.'

George slid across the wing. 'Phew, what a scorcher. We'd better look in at Customs before we go to eat. We don't want to upset the frogs unnecessarily. Follow me.'

They all walked off towards the control tower.

In the Customs Office, two French Customs officers were sitting with their feet up on their desks.

'Hello. We've just flown in from England in Oscar-November.'

'Yes, we know. What do you want?'

'We thought you might want to check our passports.'

'Monsieur, you have been watching far too much television. We do not want to see you. 'ow you say? 'ave a nice day.'

'OK guys. We've done our bit. It's about lunchtime so over to L'Escale.'

CHAPTER THIRTY

The six stood inside the restaurant waiting to be seated. The restaurant was busy. No one seemed to be taking any notice of them. They were all getting annoyed.

'Seems a bit busier than usual today.'

'Yes, perhaps we should have booked.'

'We've never needed to before.'

'No one is taking any notice of us at all.'

'It could be because we look so English? Maybe we should have hung some onions around our necks.'

'Or not washed. That would confuse them,' said George. 'Garcon, Garcon!'

A waiter stopped, turned and scowled at George.

'Are you addressing me, Monsieur?'

'Yes, I am.'

The waiter puffed himself up. 'Then that would be Maitre d'Hotel, Monsieur.'

'OK, Maitre d'Hotel, we would like a table for six people, s'iv tous plait.'

'No, George, it's s'il vous plait,' said Bob waving his hand.

'Shut up, Bob.'

''ave you booked, Monsieur?'

'No, we haven't.'

'Sacré bleu. Oh, we are extremely busy today, Monsieur, but follow me, I think I can accommodate you.'

CHAPTER THIRTY-ONE

The six now had a table but as yet no food.

'We've been sitting here ages, and still, no one has taken our order,' said Steve.

'It's such a shame, everyone told me how wonderful this restaurant was,' said Mandy 'I was really looking forward to eating here.'

'Typical bloody French,' said Guy 'They've always hated us, even though we saved them in the last war. Tell me, people, why are the avenues of Paris lined with trees?'

'I don't know Guy, but I'm sure you are going to tell us,' said Roger.

'It's so the German troops can march in the shade.'

'Well, I wouldn't mention it when the waiter finally appears Guy, or he'll probably piss in your soup. Now, are we all sure we know what we want? I'm having Moolee Frits.'

Bob had a habit of forming a circle with his thumb and forefinger and waving his hand when correcting French pronunciation. 'No, Roger. It's Moule Frites,' he said, waving his hand.

'Thanks, Bob. Perhaps you'd like to order for all of us.'

'I thought I'd try the snails,' remarked Mandy thoughtfully 'I'd like to understand why the French eat snails.'

'It's because the French don't like fast food,' said Guy.

'Oh dear, where do you get them from Guy?' asked George.

'Sorry, I must get a new scriptwriter.'

'I think I'll try the steak,' said George hungrily.

'But how would you like it done, George?' asked Bob, 'Remember bien cuit doesn't exist in France. It's either raw or almost raw.

'Just pull its horns out and wipe its arse, that will do me. I'm starving. Oh, to hell with it, I'm done waiting.'

George picked up a plate, held it under his chin, fell to his knees and shuffled through the tables to the middle of the restaurant where Maitre d'hotel is standing. The whole restaurant went quiet as everybody watched.

The Maitre d'Hotel was as cool as a cucumber. 'Can I 'elp you Monsieur?'

'Yes! Please, please can we order some food!'

'I 'ave already explained to Monsieur that we are extremely busy today,' he sighed 'but if Monsieur would like to shuffle back to 'is table, I will take the order myself.'

George turned and shuffled back to the table on his knees, still holding the plate under his chin.

He was closely followed by the Maitre d'Hotel. 'Now, Monsieur, first, what would you like to drink?'

George looked around at the others. 'I think we will have a bottle of red wine. Yes? OK, what would Maitre d'Hotel recommend?'

'May I recommend the St Emilion, Monsieur. It is full-bodied, slightly nutty with a sharp bite and leaves a bitter after-taste.'

'Sounds more like my Mother-in-law than a wine!' said Roger.

'OK, we'll try a bottle of Roger's Mother-in-law, please.'

'And what can I get you to eat?'

As one, they all grabbed Bob's right hand and held it down on the table.

'I'll have the entrecote, bien cuit.'

'I'll take the Escargot.'

'I'll have the Moule Frites.'

'I'll take the Moule Frites as well.'

'I'll try the Burger a'la Francais.'

They all released Bob's hand.

Bob took a deep breath. 'Je voudrais le marmite de trois poissons, facon bouillabaisse, quelques pommes de terre at legumes, s'il vous plait Monsieur.'

The Maitre d'Hotel was delighted. 'Oh Monsieur, votre prononciation française est très bonne. Avez-vous vécu en France ou juste visité ici souvent?

Bob looks stunned. His mouth opened and closed, but nothing came out.

'Well answer the man, Bob,' said Guy.

'I don't understand what he said!'

'But you are our French Guru, Bob. Always correcting our pronunciation. How come you don't understand?'

'Well, my brother and I bought a French course on tape. There were two tapes, one on speaking it and the other on understanding it. I took the one on speaking it. By the time I had finished that tape, my brother had lost the other one. So I never got round to understanding it.'

'Never mind Monsieur, your pronunciation is excellent! I will order your food.'

CHAPTER THIRTY-TWO

The six left the restaurant. It was sunny and extremely warm. Steve took his shirt off.

'Well, that was a cracking meal,' said George 'Does anyone want anything else to eat?'

'I'm fine,' said Steve 'I finished with a cappuccino followed by a massive brownie.'

'Well, I hope you flushed twice, you know how bad these French bogs are,' said Guy.

'You really must employ a new scriptwriter, Guy,' said George.

Mandy smacked her lips. 'My snails were lovely. I can see why the French eat them.'

'You'll be out in your garden with a torch tonight catching them,' said Roger. He grabbed Bob's arm and held it behind his back. 'My Moulee Frits were tasty.'

'Get off my arm,' said Bob.

'My steak was a bit rare--,' started George.

'Saignant,' interrupted Bob.

'Thank you, Bob. As I was saying, after I returned it, it still seemed to come back from the kitchen exactly the same.'

'I told you earlier, the Frogs don't do bien cuit. They only eat them either raw or almost raw.' He waved his hand. 'Bleu ou saignant. You might try 'tres bien cuit' next time George, but they may try to section you.'

'Thank you, Bob, I'll let you explain it all to them. As long as they remember to answer in English, you'll be fine. So everyone seems to be full, so shall we walk into town? The beach is about a mile and a half away, but the town is quite picturesque. Beautiful houses along the roads, but also a couple of short cuts through some nice wooded areas.'

CHAPTER THIRTY-THREE

'These houses are so lovely,' remarked Mandy as they walked through the town.

'Yes, this place has been the playground of the rich for many years,' said George. 'It has a casino, fine restaurants, a lovely beach and Rue St Jean is filled to the brim with market stalls. They even opened a new water sports centre right on the beach.'

'Exactly what I like about the French,' said Guy, 'They're not shy when it comes to sex. Talk about any time, any place, anywhere.'

'Not that kind of water sports, you idiot. I'm talking about wind-surfing, sailing and the like!'

'Alright, George. Easy mistake to make.'

'Oh, hang on guys, I need to stop for a bit,' said Mandy 'My sciatica is playing me up.'

'How long have you suffered from sciatica,' asked Roger.

'Ages, it's an old injury.'

'Been swinging from chandeliers?' asked Guy.

'Sciatica?' asked George 'Is that pain that goes down one leg but is actually caused by problems in your back?'

'Correct, George, I'll just squat down here for a few seconds and it'll go away.'

'Mandy, I can understand you having back problems given all that extra weight hanging off your chest, but why only pain in one leg?' asked Guy 'Is one breast much bigger than the other or something?'

Mandy got up. 'I'm not sure, Guy. Is one of your two brain cells much bigger than the other one? It certainly doesn't sound like it!'

'Now, now, guys. Calm down,' said George 'Now, this is a short-cut through a wood. It's a bit overgrown, but it takes quite a lot off the walk. Are you OK to continue Mandy?'

'Yes, I'm OK now, thanks, George.'

They entered the wood. They had to avoid overhanging branches and undergrowth. Steve put his shirt back on.

'Steve, why do you take your shirt off when you are out in the sun and put it back on again when you go into the shade?' asked Guy 'Are you too hot or too cold?'

'Neither mate, I put it back on when going into the woods because if I go home with scratches on my back, my wife will never believe I got them walking through a wood.'

'Suspicious type, is she?'

'Well, she is my second wife. She used to be my secretary. We had an affair for two years before my first wife found out. Point is that she knows all my old tricks and excuses. So you can understand why she wouldn't believe me.'

'Think yourself, lucky Guy, you never got too involved with the opposite sex,' remarked George 'They only bring problems.'

'I'll have you know that I've had ladies banging on my bedroom door at all times of the day and night.'

'I know that Guy, but they all told me they were trying to get out. You will be telling me next that you've joined the mile high club?'

'Indeed, I have George. It was on a Ryanair flight to Dublin.'

'I believe you Guy, but there has to be someone else in the toilet with you, otherwise, it doesn't count. Now if we just squeeze through this gap in the hedge, we'll find ourselves on the beach. Roger, Mandy prepare yourselves for the view.'

Mandy squeezed through the hedge. 'Oh, I see what you mean, absolutely beautiful.'

'Indeed!' said Roger, 'I'd like to come here for a holiday.'

'So would I, Roger,' said Mandy, pulling Roger towards her and kissing him, 'It's so romantic.'

Roger grabbed Mandy by the waist and lifted her up.

'Oh, hold up,' said Bob 'Sex alert!'

Guy looked at Roger and Mandy wistfully. 'I once had a girlfriend who told me sex was much better when she was on holiday. Mind you, it wasn't the best postcard I'd ever received.'

'Now we are a bit behind schedule due to the interminable wait in the restaurant,' said George 'I suggest we visit the supermarket over there to buy whatever booze, fags and perfume you want and then take a taxi back to the airport.'

'Yes,' said Mandy 'I'd rather not be late back.'

CHAPTER THIRTY-FOUR

Roger walked around the supermarket in amazement. 'Well, the French certainly know how to enjoy themselves, don't they? I've never seen so much booze in one place before.'

'Yes, they don't do things by halves. Not only French produce but lots from the rest of Europe' replied George 'I'd avoid the Greek wines though if I were you. I always find that Domestica tastes like Domestos and Retsina is a bit like Rat's piss'.

'Wow, look at these prices. So much cheaper than at home. We do so get ripped off by our government.'

'Well, don't go mad. It's unlikely we will be stopped back home but remember it all has to be for personal use. I'd avoid the

French wines because the Frogs keep all the good stuff for themselves and send all the crap up here for us daft Brits to buy.'

'I'm not buying anything, so I'll go outside and arrange a taxi,' said Bob.

'Make sure you find one that speaks English, Bob!' said Roger.

'Yes,' said Mandy 'I can't be late back.'

CHAPTER THIRTY-FIVE

Oscar-November is approaching Linton airfield.

'Linton Tower, good evening, Oscar-November,' said Steve.

'Oscar-November, Linton Tower, go ahead.'

'Oscar-November, inbound to you from Le Touquet.'

'Roger, Oscar-November. Cleared to land runway Two Six. QFE One Zero Zero Six. Wind calm.'

'Roger, Cleared to land runway Two Six. QFE One Zero Zero Six. Oscar-November.'

Mandy put her arm around Roger. 'Well, it's been a wonderful day out, I don't know how to thank you, Roger.'

'Oh, I bet you do Mandy. If you don't, I'm sure I'll think of something. Are you coming to the bar and then the Chinese?'

'No, Roger, I must get back. I should be at work, remember.'

'Yes, I forgot that. Well, today has been quite an experience for me as well. Made me even more determined to become a pilot. Pigs might fly, indeed!'

'Pigs might fly? What are you on about?'

'Oh, that's what my dear wife wrote across the front of the book you sold me about learning to fly.'

The aircraft crossed the perimeter fence of the airfield. Roger looked out the window and saw two people and two cars in the spectator's car park.

'Oh, my God,' said Roger 'Alison is waiting in the spectator's car park. What on earth?'

Mandy lent forward to look out the same window, 'Where? Oh! shit, what is worse, that's my husband Dan standing there with her. How the hell did those two meet or is it just a coincidence?'

CHAPTER THIRTY-SIX

Roger and Alison sat in the kitchen. Roger had a black eye.

'And as far as I'm concerned, you can stay in the spare room for good, Roger. I don't want you near me.'

'You never want me near you. That's the bloody trouble.'

'God knows what you might have caught from that woman. Dan told me it isn't the first time she has strayed. Makes a habit of it apparently.'

'Well, if he took more care of her obvious needs then maybe she wouldn't need to. If you took care of mine then I wouldn't need to either! So it's Dan, is it? How the hell did you two meet?'

'Quite by chance actually. It turns out we both had suspicions. She had told him she suddenly had to work on her day off, but she had come home earlier in the week with her underwear on inside out and back to front. I was sure there was more to your sudden obsession with flying than just aircraft. Going on a day trip to Le Touquet and not taking me with you? We both had decided to watch and find out what was going on, and we happened to meet in the spectator's car park.'

'How on earth did you get talking? I'm here spying on my spouse is not a recognised opening gambit between strangers.'

'We were both watching you all getting into the aircraft. He said something like 'you cow' and I asked him why he said it. It soon became apparent we had a problem in common. So we went for a coffee to discuss it. He seems a thoroughly decent man.'

'He's not all that decent. Look what he's done to my eye.'

'It's no more than you deserve Roger. I've no sympathy for you. Now I want you to promise me you won't go near the airfield again. You'll give up this silly notion of learning to fly.'

'Oh no, no. Not a chance. I had a lovely day out in Le Touquet yesterday. We got in a light aircraft and flew to France. No tickets, no airport lounges. We could have gone anywhere, the Channel Isles, Ireland or a lot further afield like Gibraltar or Malta. Flying when and where we want. Don't you realise what a fantastic hobby it is?'

'You missed out the bit about seeing the lovely Mandy every time you go there.'

'Probably unavoidable. I suppose I'll see her later, as I've got a lesson booked later this afternoon with the new Chief Flying Instructor, Lewis Davidson.'

'Oh, you are impossible Roger. Go and visit your Floozie if you must. But please stay out of my way. I'm going to work.'

Alison picked up her handbag and left the house, slamming the door. BANG!

CHAPTER THIRTY-SEVEN

'Hello Mandy,' said Roger as he walked into reception.

'Hello Roger, oh, your eye looks dreadful. Have you had anything on it?'

'Only your husband's fist.'

'Oh, I'm so sorry, Roger. He's not usually violent. Perhaps you shouldn't have called him a Eunuch.'

'Well if the cap fits, wear it, as my Mum used to say.'

'Well, the truth must have hurt.'

Roger held his hand to his eye. 'It bloody did!'

'Well, he was genuinely upset. So was your wife. What has she said?'

'Alison? Oh, she has told me not to come here any more, to give up on the idea of flying. I told her no way. The thought of being able to fly anywhere under your own steam with no queueing or tickets was what I wanted. So I'm confined to the spare room for the foreseeable future. Not that'll have any discernible effect on my sex life, but at least I won't have to listen to her snoring. What about you?'

'Much the same, I'm afraid. He wanted me to give up my job here. Keep me away from you, I suppose. But I like this job, it's not boring.'

'Well, we'll have to play it by ear, I suppose. You do still fancy me, don't you?'

'Of course, I do Roger. Yesterday's outing was brilliant. My first trip in a light aircraft and I loved it.'

'Me too. Anyway, I've got a lesson booked, presumably with the new CFI. What's he like?'

'Difficult to say. I've only met him briefly. He's in his office with his girlfriend.'

The outside door to reception opened and a rather attractive lady walked in.

'Hello, can I help you?' asked Mandy.

'Yes, I was rather hoping to learn to fly.'

'OK, well you'll need to talk to our Chief Flying Instructor, Lewis Davidson. I'll give him a buzz.'

Mandy picked up the phone just as the office door opened and the new CFI, Lewis Davidson appeared followed a woman. 'Yes, Mandy, what is it?'

'Lewis, I've got Roger here, he has a lesson booked and this lady is interested in learning to fly.'

Lewis glanced at Roger and then looked longingly at the lady. He turned to this girlfriend, 'Alright, Abigail, I'll give you a ring. See you later.'

Abigail gave him a peck on the cheek and left. Lewis walked past Roger and spoke to the lady. 'So you want to learn to fly, err sorry, I didn't catch your name?'

'It's Jane.'

'So you want to learn to fly, Jane. I always suggest a trial lesson to see how you take to it. Are you free now?'

'Well, I have to pick my son up in two hours, so is there time?'

'Oh, absolutely.'

'Lewis, Roger has a lesson booked now,' said Mandy.

Lewis turned to Roger.

'I'm sorry Roger. I'm sure you won't mind me taking Jane for a trial lesson now, will you?'

'Well, yes actually I would. I came here expecting my lesson.'

'Well, I've only been here a few hours, so I haven't had the time to read up on what training you've had so far. I'll check your records when I return, so perhaps you could book another lesson for tomorrow?'

Lewis turned and quickly propelled Jane to the door.

'Mandy, can you book us out in Hotel-Tango please.'

'Well, what a bloody cheek,' said Roger 'I've got a lesson booked, and he decides to take Jane for a trial lesson instead. Did you notice the way he looked at her? And he already has a girlfriend. Lounge Lizard or what?'

'What are you going to do?' asked Mandy.

'Can you book me another lesson for tomorrow, please. I'm not going to wait around for that snake. I think I'll go into the club for a drink. Can you join me when you finish here?'

'I don't know Roger. Dan will go mad if I'm not home on time.'

'Well, I'll leave it up to you, Mandy. Hope to see you later.'

CHAPTER THIRTY-EIGHT

Roger walked into the bar. Loud music was playing and there were lots of people he didn't recognise. The decorators had gone and the place had been given a face-lift. He stopped and looked around. He spotted Guy in the corner and walked over.

'Hello, Guy. A bit noisier today?'

'Hello, Roger. Oh, my God, he did get in a good punch last night. Your eye is terrible. That makes four black eyes in the club, and Bob has only had three of them. Not going for his record, are you?'

'Thanks, Guy. Sympathetic as usual.'

'Sorry Roger, but I've been confronted by several things after a flight abroad, you know customs, special branch and the like but never an angry husband. You've been here less than a week and you are already setting new trends.'

'The club's definitely noisier than usual today and I don't recognise any of these people. But I do like the new decor.'

'Yes, they finished it yesterday. But it was all done in a flash so Forsythe must have had it planned for some time. Trouble is, he's already opened it up to the public, as we feared he would. These arseholes are the first but once word spreads about the late licence, you can imagine what will happen. On the plus side though, I've got more work out of it. A disco every night plus a grab-a-granny night on Sundays.'

'Well, it's an ill wind as they say. I'm pleased for you, Guy.'

'Such a brilliant trip yesterday, wasn't it? Well, apart from the ending, obviously. When George went across the restaurant on his knees and begged for food, I thought I'd die laughing. He's got some bottle!'

'I thought Steve putting his shirt on every time he went through the undergrowth was funny. All because he couldn't go home with scratches on his back? I've obviously led a sheltered life.'

'Well, not that sheltered. How are things with Mandy now? Dan wasn't pleased when you called him a eunuch, was he? He must have given her some stick when they got home.'

'I think we both got some stick when we got home. We'll have to play it by ear, I suppose. I did ask her to join me here when she finishes, but she wasn't keen. Anyway, I need a drink. Is Chantelle still here?'

'Oh yes, Chantelle is still here, bless her little cotton socks. I'm surprised she is, as she has taken so much abuse from customers. But she won't cope if we get many more drunken arseholes in though. They don't like waiting for their next alcohol fix.'

'I'll go and say hello. Can I get you one, Guy?'

'Thanks, Roger. I'll have a black eye cocktail.'

'Are you making that up?'

'No, I'm not making it up. It's a cocktail built around Rye whisky. But I am taking the piss. Pint of bitter please.'

Roger went to the bar. Chantelle came over.

'Cor, what a shiner mate! But hang on, I remember you. You was the one I threatened to punch the other day when you insulted me. Seems you make a habit of it, but you got your just deserts this time.'

'Have you finished? I thought you were here to serve drinks, not as an amateur psychologist. Two pints of bitter please, and less of your lip.'

Chantelle scowled at him and started to pour. Roger looked around the bar in horror at the customers and their antics. Some were laughing loudly and at the end of the bar, a group were sticking lighted matches into bottles.

'Ten pounds,' said Chantelle.

'Ten pounds? Bloody extortion!' replied Roger.

He put ten pounds on the bar and returned with the beer. Guy had been joined by another man.

He handed a beer to Guy who drank half in one go. 'Thanks, Roger, I really needed that. Now I'd like you to meet Miles, he's been out in Thailand for a while flying helicopters. Miles, meet Roger. He's learning to fly.'

'Nice to meet you, Roger,' said Miles 'Say, mate looks like you've been in the wars with that eye. Whatever does the other bloke look like?'

'I didn't hit him back. My parents taught me not to hit women and eunuchs.'

'Oh, right. An affair of the heart, was it? Enough said old boy. If you're having trouble getting your leg over, you should come to Thailand. Eastern women certainly know how to pleasure a man. It's a bit like a Stanley Kubrick war film out there.'

Miles put on a high-pitched eastern woman's voice. 'Hello Johnny, only five dollars, me love you long time.'

'I wasn't having trouble getting my leg over. I was actually living the life of Riley. Unfortunately, Riley caught me and punched me. Besides, I hear half of the prostitutes in Thailand are really men?'

'Well it's true you have to be careful. It can be difficult to tell the difference until you get between the sheets and then you find out you've got matching wedding tackle. I nearly got caught out once. Gorgeous looking girl. It was only when we got back to her place, and she reversed into a tiny garage at the first attempt that I thought, hang on a minute and did a runner. Now tell me, what the hell has happened to the old club?'

'Jed sold it to Forsythe,' said Guy. 'He's made a brilliant job doing it up but then opened it up to Joe public, hence all the arseholes milling around. On the plus side, I get to do a disco every night and a grab-a-granny night on Sundays.'

'Well if the arseholes don't shut the club down, I'm sure your disco will Guy!' said Miles with a laugh. 'Seriously though, mate, good luck with it. Well, I only popped in to see who was around. I'll have more time to visit later in the week. Nice to meet you, Roger. See you around, Guy.'

Miles left and Guy drank the other half of his beer down in one gulp. 'Haven't seen him in ages. Another drink, Roger?'

'Err, I haven't finished this one yet, but OK I'll have another pint of bitter, please. What's with you drinking like a fish today?' asked Roger.

'I'm celebrating my new job. I feel lucky today.'

CHAPTER THIRTY-NINE

Guy picked up his glass and went to the bar. There was a commotion going on between Chantelle and what looked like a very pretty Eastern European lady. Some drunken customers were joining in.

'I want cock.'

'Come outside with me, love, I'll give you cock.'

'No, No, I want cock to drink.'

'You can have a drink from mine, love.'

'Whoa, fellows,' said Guy 'I think what this lady wants is a coke to drink, Chantelle. Can you sort that and two pints of bitter please.'

'Well, why don't she just say so?' muttered Chantelle.

'It's her Eastern European accent.'

'Yes, yes, that is what I want. A cock to drink.'

'Look love, you pronounce it COKE. COKE. Say I want a COKE to drink.'

'I want a cock to drink.'

'No! You want a COKE to drink.'

'What is difference between cock and coke?'

'Well, probably not a lot if you shake the bottle before you take the top off.'

'I not understand. But thank you for help. My name is Enis. What is yours?'

'My name is Guy.'

'Ah, I remember. You blew up Parliament, yes?'

'No. I didn't. I would like to but what you are thinking of was four hundred-odd years ago.'

Chantelle returned with their drinks. 'Two pints of bitter, and a cock. Fourteen pounds, please.'

'Fourteen pounds? Bloody hell.'

''ow much to pay?' asked Enis.

'No, that's OK. I'll get it,' replied Guy 'But please remember to say "I want a COKE" in future. A cock is something entirely different!'

'So what is cock?'

'Err well, if you go outside with any of those arseholes over there, you will find out the hard way! And I mean hard!'

Guy took the drinks back to Roger.

'So what was all the commotion about?' asked Roger.

'The girl is Eastern European,' replied Guy 'She kept asking for cock rather than coke. I put her right.'

'That was nice of--,' Roger stopped. Another commotion had broken out.

CHAPTER FORTY

Two men were shouting and squaring up to each other. A third man was trying to break it up.

'You take that back you bastard or I'll flatten you.'

'Oh, piss off you. You couldn't punch your way out of a paper bag.'

'Come on guys, break it up now.'

'No, I'm going to smash this bastard's face, what the f--?'

Chantelle had come from behind the bar and grabbed his collar and belt. She lifted him off his feet and took him to the door. 'Right. You are out and you are barred. If I see you in here again, I won't be so gentle with you.'

She pushed him outside and returned to a round of applause from the members.

'Wow,' said Roger 'When she threatened to punch me, I didn't take her seriously. I'd better be careful in future!'

The third man staggered over in a drunken and distressed state. 'She's thrown me mate out!'

'Yes, we saw,' said Roger 'He was starting a fight.'

'There was no need to throw him out.'

'I think there was every need. We come here to enjoy ourselves, not to fight.'

'Bloody woman. I hate women. Women are always trouble. Did you know the word woman is actually an acronym? It stands for Wicked, Orible, Mean, And, Nasty.'

'Well, I suggest you go and tell Chantelle that, if you dare, err, sorry I don't know your name?'

'I'm Vic. I'm from Hull.'

'Hull? So what brings you to Linton?'

'I work at the plant hire firm on the industrial estate. It's based in Hull. I'm in charge of the Portaloos. Emptying and cleaning them when they come back off-site, and then shifting them back to the ready for hire section. They call me Mister Shitfer Man.'

'Why?' asked Guy 'Because you must have shit for brains to do a job like that?'

'No Guy,' replied Roger, 'I think you just swap the f and the t round in Mr Shifter.'

'Oh, I see,' said Guy 'Silly me. So I haven't seen you in here before Vic. How did you find out about it?'

'We had a leaflet through the door at work, so we thought we would give it a try. Only a tenner membership, and a late licence. Oh, and a disco as well but not a very good one, so they say. DJ thinks he's Prince Charles or something. When does that start?'

'Actually, I shall be starting it shortly.'

'Oops, sorry, my turn to be silly! Perhaps they'll rename this the Shitfer Club because they've got shit for a DJ! Good evening.'

Vic laughed and returned to his remaining friend.

CHAPTER FORTY-ONE

'Well, what an enlightening conversation,' said Roger, 'I think I'll call him Vic from Hell rather than Vic from Hull.'

'I've got to get ready for my disco now Roger,' said Guy 'See you later.'

'Good luck. I'm going to get another pint.'

Roger went to the bar. Chantelle came over.

'Pint of bitter, please Chantelle.'

'Come to be rude again, have you?'

'Not bloody likely. I watched you throw the drunk out. Where did you learn to do that?'

'My brother is a bouncer at a night club. He taught me. If you grab them from behind by the collar and belt, lift them off the ground then they are sort of helpless. Leave the drink in their hand as it makes it more difficult for them to grab anything on the way out.'

She put his pint on the bar. 'Five pounds please.'

'Well respect where respect is due. I think you make a better bouncer than a barmaid though.'

Roger picked his pint up and spotted George limping into the club.

'You can't resist being rude, can you?' said Chantelle 'Would you like another black eye to match that one?'

'Another black eye, Roger?' said George, 'I think one is enough. Unless your name is Bob, of course. Wow, that is a nasty one. Pint of bitter, please Chantelle.'

'Hello, George. Did I just see you limping?'

'Yes. The gout is playing me up again. It's so painful that when you lay in bed, you can't even have a sheet touch your toe'

'Have you tried Viagra?'

'What, for gout?'

'Yes. It'll certainly help to keep the sheet off your toe!'

'Ha bloody ha. Got that one off of Guy, I suppose. Well the club decor is certainly better, which is more than can be said for some new members.'

'Yes, we've already had one fight situation which Chantelle managed to sort out.'

'Chantelle?'

'Yes, she picked the guy up by his belt and collar and threw him out. Brother is a bouncer apparently, so she knows all the tricks.'

Chantelle put George's pint on the bar.

'Five pounds please.'

George put a fiver on the bar.

'Extortionate.'

'Well don't moan at me. I just work here.'

'I wouldn't dare. You might throw me out.'

'See the idiot over there that's acting the fool, George,' said Roger 'he is Vic from Hell. We met him earlier.'

'From hell?'

'From Hull, actually. But hell seems more appropriate. He cleans out Portaloos for a living.'

'Oh, that doesn't bear thinking about. The smell of those things on my site after builders have had eight pints and a Vindaloo the night before, you just wouldn't believe. I hope he had a shower before coming in here.

Anyway, how is flying going? I think you said you had a lesson booked today.'

'Yes, I did. But the new Chief Flying Instructor, what's his name, Lewis Davidson, he got a better offer. Some smart bird came in wanting to learn to fly, so he cancelled me, and took her out for a trial lesson. He's already got a girlfriend, so he seems a bit of a fanny maggot to me.'

'Oh dear, that's not on is it! Most unprofessional. Sounds a right git.'

In the background, Guy was starting his disco evening.

CHAPTER FORTY-TWO

'Hello and good evening, Ladies and Gentlemen,' said Guy in his Prince Charles voice, inter dispersed with music, 'Welcome to the Cloud Nine Disco with me, your host, Prince Charles.'

'Guy shouldn't be doing a disco tonight,' said George.

'Indeed,' said Roger 'But now Forsythe has opened it up to all and sundry, Guy is doing a disco every night, with a grab-a-granny night on Sundays. Let's find a seat and sit down.'

'You may be wondering why I'm doing a disco while I'm heir to the throne. It's because it's so bloody boring being Prince Charles. I've implored Mother to abdicate, but she tells me I will succeed to the throne

in the normal manner. Over her dead body.
Now just a minute, I must put this headgear
on.'

Guy put on a fox hat.

'There. I promised Mother I'd wear it. We
were sitting at breakfast this morning, and
she asked me "Charles, what are you doing
today?". I replied that I was doing a disco
this evening at the Linton Flying Club. She
said "Linton? Linton? Wear the fox hat?." So
let's kick off this evening with an
appropriate number for a flying club. It's
The Byrd's, Eight Miles High.'

Eight Miles High started to play. Guy sat
down. Enis came over.

''ello again, Guy.'

'Hello, Enis'

'Can I sit with you, plis?'

'Yes of course. Pull up a chair.'

'Thank you. I like you Guy, you are a nice
man, not like those out there.'

'Thanks.'

'They are so rude out there. I took your
advice but they were so rude.'

'My advice? What do you mean?'

'I asked you what was cock. And you said,
if I go outside with any of those arseholes
then I will find out.'

'No! No! That wasn't advice. That was a bloody warning.'

'Oh well, I asked a man, and we went outside as you said and I found out. No, how you say, romance, no kissing, he just flopped it out. So now I know. Cock is Pula. That is what we call it in Romania. Like you say, I found out the 'ard way.'

Guy was horrified. 'Oh no. I'm so sorry. I thought you understood English better than you do.'

'It is OK. No problem. I have seen pula many times before. I like pula. Now I have learnt new words, cock and coke. Thank you for helping me. I must not mix them up.'

'Best not to. There are lots of strange people around these days. Well, now you know.'

'Are you married, Guy?'

'Me? No.'

'Have you a girlfriend?'

'No, not at the moment.'

'Well, I would like to be your girlfriend. Do you like me?'

'Yes, of course, I do. You are very pretty. Hang on, I need to change the record.'

Guy stood up.

'That was the Byrds and their 1968 hit 'Eight Miles high'. Continuing with the flying theme it's Jefferson Airplane with their 1967 hit 'Somebody to Love'. Well, I need someone to love, I've only got Camilla, and she looks like a bloody horse.'

'You are so funny, Guy.'

'Thanks.'

'I like the words to this song. I need someone to love. Do you need somebody to love, Guy? I need somebody to love and I think it's you.'

Enis pulled Guy towards her and they kissed.

CHAPTER FORTY-THREE

Roger and Alison were having breakfast.

'How about another cup of tea?' asked Roger.

'You know where the kettle is, Roger' replied Alison.

'Yes, OK, I do.'

'You could always get your Floozie to make you one.'

'Yes dear, I could. But I don't want her to make me a cup of tea. I don't want to have a bloody Floozie. I want a normal relationship with my wife. But it doesn't seem to be available.'

'Well, my gynaecologist did say I shouldn't have sex for a while.'

'Really? What did your dentist say?'

'Roger! No more of your filth please!'

'But if you've got a blockage up there, then perhaps I should get Gynorod to come round and take a look?'

'Roger!! You are impossible. I'm off to work.'

'I'm sorry, I'm sorry. I know I shouldn't react like that, but it's so bloody frustrating.'

'Well, you'll have to go see your Floozie then, see what her dentist said. My bet is she has false teeth, so she can take them out. Now I'm off to work. I'll be working late tonight, not that I expect you'll be here or would even notice if you were. Goodbye.'

Alison stormed out and slammed the door. BANG!

Roger sighed and switched the kettle on. He sat down and started to read aloud from a book about meteorology.

'Clouds form when warm, moist air rises into cooler air and is eventually cooled below its dew point. The air can no longer hold the moisture as water vapour and it condenses as actual droplets of water which forms the cloud.'

In the background, the kettle was boiling furiously and a cloud was forming. Roger eventually noticed, sprung up and switched it off.

He stared at the cloud. 'Ah, now I understand.'

As the steam cleared, Roger caught sight of the kitchen clock. 'Time for my lesson'.

CHAPTER FORTY-FOUR

Mandy was looking after reception as Roger walked in.

'Hello Roger, how's tricks?'

'Oh much the same, pretty icy. How about you?'

'Yes, that sums it up for me as well.'

'You didn't join me in the club last night.'

'No, well I did say I had to be home. I wish I had, did you hear what happened to Guy?'

'Guy? No? He was in the club last night doing a disco. That Romanian girl Enis seems to have taken a shine to him and was all over him like a rash. So what happened?'

'Yes, that all makes sense now. Well, apparently he got lucky with Enis and took her home. Things must have really got hot in the bedroom because he fell off the bed and cut his head open on a radiator. It must have been serious because an ambulance attended and Guy ended up in A and E.'

Roger smiled broadly. 'Wow, the dirty, lucky bastard. Enis is quite a looker.'

'Oh, a looker, is she? And I'm not I suppose?'

'What? Of course, you are. Doesn't stop Enis being a looker as well. So poor old Guy, it got so intense he falls off the bed and bangs his head on a radiator. Not the sort of bang he had in mind, I'm sure. So how do you know this? Is he still in the hospital?'

'No, he had some stitches, and they sent him home. I only found out because my next-door neighbour was the ambulance driver, and he knew we worked at the same place.'

'Well, I'm sure he shouldn't have told you. Data protection or something similar. He would be in a lot of trouble if the hospital found out. But I'm glad he did tell you. What a story. Guy has really shot up in my estimation. Now about my lesson. Am I going to get one today?'

'Well, you are booked in but Lewis is in his office with Jane, you know the lady who came in and stole your lesson. When they got back yesterday, they spent a lot of time in his office before they left. And he turned up with her again this morning.'

'Did he now? He's a fast worker, I'll give him that.'

'Would you like me to give him a call and remind him?'

'Yes, please do.'

Mandy picked up the phone. 'Hello, Lewis. Roger is here for his lesson. OK, thanks.'

Mandy puts the phone down. 'He says he'll be out in a minute.'

The door to Lewis's office opened and Jane and Lewis appeared.

Jane kissed him on the lips. 'I'll see you later, Lewis.'

'I'll look forward to it,' said Lewis with a smile.

Lewis turned to Roger and Mandy who are watching open-mouthed.

'Hello, Roger. Sorry about yesterday, but I didn't want to turn a potential customer away, and anyway I hadn't had time to review your training.'

'I see,' said Roger 'Do you snog all your potential customers or only the good-looking ones?'

'And weren't you snogging another lady yesterday?' pointed out Mandy 'Abigail, if I recall correctly?'

'What is this?' Lewis was quite taken aback 'An episode of the Moral Maze? I don't see any of that concerns either of you. Now, Roger, I see you have mastered all the basics, so now I think it's time to start you on circuit training, you know, take-offs and landings. Then, when I think you are safe enough, you can go solo. How are you doing with your Ground Studies? You do need to pass Air Law first.'

'Yes, I think I am OK with Air Law. It's meteorology I'm struggling a bit with. But when I boiled the kettle this morning, a few things fell into place.'

'When you think you can pass Air Law, let me know and you can sit the paper. Now let's go and start on the circuit. Mandy, can you book us out in Hotel-Tango, please.'

'OK, Lewis, will do.'

CHAPTER FORTY-FIVE

Hotel-Tango sped down runway two six at Linton Airfield.

'At 65 knots, gently pull back on the control column' said Lewis to Roger. 'That's it. Hold that attitude. At five hundred feet, start a ninety-degree climbing turn to the left.' Roger was enjoying every minute.

'At one thousand feet level off. Now hold the nose down and let the speed build up to 90 knots,' continued Lewis 'now throttle back to twenty-two hundred rpm. Trim for straight and level. Now check for other aircraft and turn downwind. OK. Now call downwind.'

Roger pressed the PTT switch and hoped it wouldn't stick. 'Hotel-Tango, downwind.'

'Roger, Hotel-Tango. Cleared to finals, number one,' replied Linton Tower.

'Cleared to finals, number one. Hotel-Tango.'

'Right, now we do our landing checks,' said Lewis 'Brakes are off, undercarriage down and welded, mixture is rich, carburettor heat to hot, fuel pump on, hatches and harnesses secure, carburettor heat back to cold. Now we are far enough downwind, look back and get that airfield perspective in your mind. Now check for other aircraft and turn base leg. Reduce the power to fifteen hundred rpm to descend, hold the nose up to reduce the speed to 70 knots, trim for that speed. Now anticipate the turn on to finals at about five hundred feet, and tell ATC you are on finals.'

'Hotel-Tango, finals.'

'Roger Hotel-Tango. Cleared touch and go runway two six, Wind Two Six Zero at five knots.'

'Cleared touch and go, Hotel-Tango.'

'Now keep the speed at 65 knots using the elevators and control the rate of descent with the power. Keep the view of the nose just short of the threshold. Now as we pass over the threshold reduce the power slightly, use the elevators to bring the nose up and thus the speed back, and aim to land at about 60 knots on the main wheels, that's it, now gently lower the nose, and we're down. Now increase the power to maximum, and we're off again. Well done, Roger.'

CHAPTER FORTY-SIX

Roger and Lewis walked back into reception.

'Well, that wasn't bad for a first attempt, Roger,' said Lewis 'Take-offs, reasonable. Circuits reasonable but you need to nail the speed and rate of descent on final approach. But that will come with practise. See you next lesson.'

'OK, Lewis. Thank you.'

Lewis disappeared back into his office and shut the door.

'Well, I enjoyed that. I almost landed it myself. Great fun.'

'Sounds like you'll make a pilot yet, Roger.'

'I think I'll celebrate with a drink in the bar. Fancy joining me later?'

'Well, I probably can. Dan said he was working late tonight, so he won't be home at the usual time.'

'Excellent. Perhaps you can borrow the keys to the executive jet again?'

'Oh, I'm not sure Roger. I felt so sorry for Mr Hamilton, he had to pay for an engineer to inspect his aircraft.'

'Don't worry, I've got a blanket in my car. I'll see you in the bar later.'

'OK, Roger.'

CHAPTER FORTY-SEVEN

Roger walked into the bar. There were a couple of noisy groups of men enjoying themselves. Roger saw Captain Slack and his crew near the bar.

Sandy spotted him. 'Hello Roger Moore, can I buy you a drink?'

'Thank you, Sandy. I'll have a pint please.'

'Chantelle, pint of bitter for Roger, please.'

Chantelle made a croaking noise in response.

'So how are you, Sandy?'

'Oh, fair to piddling, thanks. How's the flying going?'

'Great, thanks. Started circuit training today.'

Chantelle arrived with Roger's pint.

'Well, I'm sure you'll soon be going solo.'

'Not a problem. With my wife, I'm always having to go solo!'

'Oh, dear. That's not good. Now your instructor will let you do a few good circuits on your own without his intervention, then he'll jump out and ask you to do one circuit and come back for him. Don't worry when then happens, your instructor won't let you go until he's really sure you'll be safe. You may just find it a little odd with an empty right-hand seat.'

'Thanks for the information. Now I'm puzzled why the captain of an aircraft always sits on the left. In a car, the driver sits on the right.'

'Ah, well that's because the co-pilot is usually young and after the Hostesses. He sits on the right so the big flashy watch on his left wrist is very visible. The captain is much older and is far more concerned with damaging his watch on the centre consul, so he sits on the left.'

'Is that really true?'

'I'm not sure, but when you fly every day with Kyle, you tend to pick up his silly stories.'

Kyle heard his name being mentioned and joined them.

'Did I hear my name being taken in vain? Hello Duckie, how's your belly off for spots?'

'Probably OK, thanks Kyle. We were just discussing your unlikely stories.'

'They're all true, I swear. Come on Sandy, the crew bus is here. Sorry, Roger, we are all off now.'

'I was going to buy Sandy another drink.'

'Some other time, Roger, I'd really like that. Bye for now.'

The crew all left the club. Roger looked around and spotted Hugh, the customs officer, further along the bar.

'Hello, I can't remember your name, but I think I met you when we went to Le Touquet.'

'Yes Roger, you did. I'm Hugh.'

'Ah yes, Hugh. Now I remember. Personal use Hugh.'

'I obviously made an impression, if you remember personal use.'

'Well, I'm new to all this, so I try hard to remember what people tell me.'

'We are not as bad as we seem, but we do need to preserve some rules. Mostly, we look for drugs and drug dealers. We check private flights, but we also check airline crews as well. We had a problem with Kyle last week.'

'Kyle? Why?'

'We found a false bottom in his suitcase.'

'Really? What was in it?'

'Oops, sense of humour failure, Roger. I'll give you a clue. There was nothing in it when we found it, but he would probably be in it himself later on. Now I've got to go back to work. See you soon.'

Hugh walked off and left Roger puzzled.

'I don't understand. How could he get into the bottom of a suitcase?'

CHAPTER FORTY-EIGHT

Mandy crept into the club and goosed Roger. 'Hello, big boy!'

'What the--? Oh, it's you, Mandy.'

'Who did you expect?'

'Well, only you, I suppose although sometimes, the way Kyle looks at me--'

'Oh, you think Kyle is gay, do you?'

'Well let's just say I think he might help them out if they were short-handed! Now can I buy you a drink?'

'I'll have a G and T, please.'

'Chantelle, can I have another pint and a G and T please.'

Chantelle makes the croaking noise again.

Guy entered the club. He had a bandage around his head.

'Can you make that two bitters please Chantelle, Guy's here. Hello Guy, that radiator must have been enormous to do that sort of damage!'

Guy was dumbfounded, 'What?? How the hell did you hear about that?'

'Well, you've heard the old expression 'walls have ears'?'

'Yes.'

'Well, radiators do too. And mouths as well, so they can tell of sexual hi-jinx performed with young Romanian ladies. I take my hat off to you mate. It must have been some steamy session.'

'How the hell do you know all that?'

'If I told you that, I'd have to kill you. Don't worry about it, your reputation in the club here is going to soar. People will soon be asking you for sex advice.'

'Oh' said Guy, warming to the idea 'Well I don't know how you found all that out, but yes it was a bit steamy. These foreign girls could teach our English girls a thing or two. Do you know that they...'

'Yes Guy, we believe you,' said Mandy 'Just spare us the blow-by-blow account.'

'There you are, Mandy. You knew already.'

'Are you going to do your disco with the bandage on your head?' asked Roger.

'I suppose I'll have to. They told me to leave it on for at least a week.'

George entered the club and joined them. 'Hello everybody. Guy, what the hell have you got on your head? Are you doing a Sikh themed disco tonight?'

'No, George,' said Roger 'Guy had a sexual accident.'

'A sexual accident? I've heard of giving head, but I thought that was something quite different.'

'Do you remember the stunning Romanian girl that said she wanted cock when she really meant coke?'

'Yes.'

'Well, Guy gave it to her.'

'I'm confused now. How did Guy end up with a head injury buying her a coke?'

'No, George. He got a head injury giving her cock. They had a steamy sex session and Guy fell off the bed and smashed his head on a radiator.'

'Wow Guy, you dark horse. Respect. Can you come round and give my missus some ideas? I've got two radiators in my bedroom, might double my chances. Let me buy everyone a drink to celebrate Guy's good luck. Who wants what?'

'Well, that's two pints of bitter, a G and T, and whatever you are having George.'

'OK. Chantelle can I have three pints of bitter and a G and T, please.'

Chantelle croaked again.

'Sorry, I didn't catch that,' said George.

Chantelle croaked again, 'I said is that a slimline tonic?'

'Yes, I think so. Why are you croaking like that?'

'I've got a sore throat.'

'That's no problem. I've got some cream for that.'

Chantelle looked puzzled, a look which quickly changed to a thoughtful look as she considered options. Then a look of horror came over her face as she realised what he meant. Chantelle turned, coughed and spat in the sink. She poured the drinks shaking her head in disbelief.

'I can't believe you just said that, George,' said Roger.

'I can't believe you even thought it, George,' said Mandy.

'Until last night, I never believed it could happen,' said Guy.

'Well, I'm pleased it did Guy. Chantelle didn't seem too pleased at the prospect though did she?'

'To be fair George, you are old enough to be her Father'

'More like her bloody Grandfather,'

'Steady Guy, you don't want two visits to A and E in one day, do you?'

'No, sorry George, I meant elder brother!'

Chantelle returned and puts the drinks on the bar. 'That'll be twenty-three pounds please.'

'Extortion,' said George 'So Roger, did you have your lesson today? '

'Yes, George. But that Lewis Davidson is a real lounge lizard, yesterday he was kissing Abigail goodbye after Jane came in, today he's kissing Jane goodbye.'

'And last night after they got back from the trial lesson, they spent ages in his office,' said Mandy 'then this morning, he turns up with her first thing.'

'Wow. What a week. Roger and Mandy, Guy and Enis and now Lewis and Jane,' said George 'We'll have to change the name to Linton Sex Club if this continues. Perhaps Forsythe has put something in the beer. Apart from water that is.'

CHAPTER FORTY-NINE

A group of four men entered the bar. They are already drunk.

Roger recognises one of them. 'Oh no. It's Vic from Hell.'

'Oh that idiot from yesterday,' said George 'Watch out, here he comes.'

'Hello, I'm Vic. Remember me from yesterday?'

'Could we ever forget? How are you?'

Vic's mobile started to ring. Vic looked at the phone.

'I'm banging, mate. Oh, hold on, it's the bloody wife.'

'Wow, you actually have a wife?'

'Yeah. Susie. She can't get enough of me. I brought her down here for a few days. Hang on.'

He fiddled with the phone and turned the loudspeaker on.

'Hello darling,' said Vic.

'Where the hell are you, Vic?' asked Susie.

'I'm just having a drink with some friends on the way home, my darling.'

'Well, what's the point of bringing me all this way down south, leaving me in a caravan all day and then not coming home as soon as you can?'

'I won't be long, my dear. You'll be alright.'

'Be alright? Be alright? I'm bored and I'm pissed off. If you don't come home now, you ain't getting it up my arse tonight. Goodbye!'

Susie hung up. Everyone was aghast.

Vic looked around, 'She loves me really. She'll be OK.'

Vic staggered off back to his friends. No one said anything for a while.

'Sorry, I'm absolutely speechless,' said Mandy 'That is the worst conversation I've ever listened to. That poor woman brought down here and left in a caravan all day on her own, and then he goes on the piss with his mates at night. I could cry for her. Absolutely awful.'

She looked at Guy who seemed transfixed. 'Guy, will you stop staring at my breasts, please.'

'I'm not staring at your breasts. I was just thinking what a kind, warm heart you have. Not my fault if your tits are in front of your heart is it?'

'I was really amazed he even had a wife,' said George 'I'm absolutely gob-smacked now.'

'So how is the gout George?' asked Guy 'I didn't notice you limping tonight.'

'No, not so much. The Doctor increased my dose of Allopurinol. Seems to have sorted it. Anyway, you didn't finish telling me about your flying Roger?

'I started circuit training today. But the wife is still dead against it. Did your family object when you started flying George?'

'Well the wife was OK, but my father and grandfather weren't at all keen. It seems I'm descended from a long line of seamen.'

'Well, if you think about it, George, I suppose we're all descended from a long line of semen,' said Guy thoughtfully.

'Oh Guy, that was awful,' said Mandy 'Go wash your mouth out.'

Guy looked at her. 'Do you w--'

'If you say what I think you are going to say, Guy,' interrupted Mandy 'I promise you I'll punch your lights out. Three visits to A and E in one day?'

'Oh well. Look I need to go and start my disco now. Anybody got any requests?'

'Yes. Don't switch the amplifier on.'

'Yes. Don't speak into the microphone.'

'Don't touch the turntable.'

'I'll take that as a no then,' said Guy 'See you--'

'Guy!' Guy! 'ow are you. 'ow is your head?' interrupted Enis, appearing from nowhere.

She grabbed him and kissed him on the lips.

'I'm OK thanks, Enis. All the better for that kiss.'

'Oh, I am so sorry Guy. I get carried away last night--'

'--and I got carried away but on a stretcher! Now I'm just going to start my disco, so why don't we continue this conversation on the stage. Away from wagging ears.'

Suddenly Roger started to laugh.

'What's so funny?' asked Mandy.

'I've just realised what Hugh meant. He told me they had found a false bottom in Kyle's suitcase. I didn't get it. But the penny just dropped. A false bottom! He even gave me a clue. He said there was nothing in it when they found it, but Kyle would probably be in it later on. I didn't understand.'

'Well you seem to have got it now, whatever it was,' said George 'I just hope it's not catching.'

'Anyone fancy another drink?' asked Roger.

'No, I've got to drive home, and I usually start to feel a bit light-headed after two G and Ts,' said Mandy 'Strangely I'm fine tonight as if I hadn't had as much.'

'Forsythe has probably been watering the bloody gin down, so he makes more profit,' said George 'the beer as well, I wouldn't be surprised. Sort of thing he would do.'

Roger turned and looked at the optics behind the bar. 'Well you wouldn't notice water in most spirits, would you. The colour I mean. Gin and vodka are both clear so it would be indistinguishable. Hang on, the optics say twenty-five millilitres. I'm sure that they used to say thirty-five millilitres. I'd put money on it.'

'You're right,' said George 'I know for a fact that Jed always served thirty-five millilitres shots. That bastard Forsythe has not only upped the bloody prices, but he's also reduced the bloody measures as well.'

A lot of shouting started in the bar, as two men square up to each other.

'And he's never here to face the music is he?' remarked George 'I'm going to come in here one morning and catch him. Give him a piece of my mind. Excuse me, call of nature.' George left for the toilet.

Mandy put her arms around Roger. 'Nice to be alone with you at last.'

'Yes, it is. Not sure about all this fuss going on though.'

Chantelle left the bar and tried to calm things down. But one thug punched another and the bar descended into fighting.

'Oh my God, it's all kicked off. Definitely time to leave.'

'Yes, I don't like this. Please let's get out of here now.'

Roger and Mandy circumnavigated the trouble and headed for the door.

CHAPTER FIFTY

Mandy and Roger emerged from the club.

'Have you got the keys to the jet?'

'Yes. Have you got the blanket?'

'Yes, it's in my car.'

They collected the blanket from the car and walked over to the executive jet just as two vans of police arrived at the club.

'I think we are well out of that.'

'Yes. I can't believe how much the club has changed in a week.'

They climbed into the aircraft and shut the door.

'This is so nice Roger. I wish I was married to you and not Dan.'

'Yes. I wish I was married to you and not Alison. That's the trouble. Marriage is like a game of cards. In the beginning, all you need is two hearts and a diamond. By the end, you just wish you had a club and a spade.'

'Did you say Dan was working late tonight?'

'Yes, I did. It's unusual.'

'Alison said she was working late tonight as well. That's very unusual. Alison told me she and Dan got on well together. You don't suppose--'

TO BE CONTINUED.